CELT

Robert F Lyons

CONTENTS

CHAPTER ONE

THE AWAKENING

Timothy sat on a fallen tree trunk to rest. He'd been tramping around for about two hours with his metal detector in his favourite place: 'Tarbock wood', a very old wood about a mile or so from his home in Hough Green. Timothy was thirteen and he spent a lot of time on his own, he didn't get on very well at school as he had been bullied since he started at St Joseph's comprehensive, even by some of the girls. He was also rather unhappy at home, as his stepfather was a violent drunkard and Timothy stayed out of his way as much as possible, especially when his stepfather had been drinking, which was quite often. He cursed the day his mother had married him as they had both been on the wrong end of his violent temper at one time or another. Timothy's own father had died when he was about three, so he didn't remember much about him.

He felt at home in his favourite wood, he enjoyed his time searching for old coins and other metal objects and dreaming about whom they once belonged to. He looked around and gazed at the varieties of trees: Ash, Oak, Sycamore and Horse Chestnut, he smiled as he thought about how they all seemed to get on together and flourish. It was a place where Tim felt comfortable, as if he was meant to be there. It was nevertheless a very strange place, there were few birds singing there and he saw no animals there. It was in fact rather dark and very quiet in that wood. He didn't understand how or why he felt so comfortable in that place, but he did. He was sat in a small clearing. No trees for a few yards all around, but lots of weeds and nettles, he often ended up here as there was a wide pathway about fifty yards long that seemed to lead to it, over a stone bridge that was barely visible because of the overgrown bushes and grass. The bridge crossed over a rather deep and fast flowing stream, it was too deep and dangerous to cross otherwise. It was very secluded there and it was obvious that very few people ever ventured into the place, apart from Tim, he spent a lot of time there. In fact, it was quite a scary place, but Tim didn't really think so, he felt good when he was in that place.

After resting for a while timothy decided it was time to go home so he reached down to pick up his detector, when he accidentally hit the switch and turned the thing on, he then noticed that it was bleeping to indicate that there was some metal object underneath. He took his trowel out of his shoulder bag and started to scrape away the dead leaves and soil from where his feet had been. As he picked up a heavy object, it was covered in muck and just looked like a piece of stone. Chipping off the muck with his trowel it started to look and sound like metal. He took out a wire brush, and began scrubbing at the object, which started to shine; it was looking like bronze. Tim sat back down on the log as he cleaned his find further, when he received the most bizarre shock. It was like a bolt of lightning, and he ended up on his back on the other side of the log. Dazed and bewildered Tim picked himself up off the leafy earth. As he stumbled to his feet, he became aware of a strange figure a few feet in front of him. Tim blinked and wiped his eyes. He couldn't believe what he was looking at. A large blonde man almost naked, his body covered in some kind of paint, blue and green, his hair, though it was obviously blonde, it was stood up on end as if he had suffered an electric shock, and it was covered in some white substance. It was by far the most frightening sight Timothy had ever seen. "Ah!" Tim shouted, as he focussed on the stranger and realised, he was really there. "Who are you, and where did you come from?" Tim said nervously. The stranger spoke, but Tim couldn't understand a word he was saying, it was just a garbled noise, some strange language, Tim had heard nothing like it before. Then the weirdest thing happened; Tim could understand what the man was saying, without knowing the language. The man's thoughts were coming into Tim's head. He told Tim not to be afraid, because he was in no danger from him.

"Who are you?" Tim repeated. The strange man stared at Tim and smiled, "I am Vortan!" he replied. "Vortan, I've never heard that name before, where did you come from?" Tim said nervously. "I come from right here!" said the man, laughing. "Well, I've never seen you before and I spend a lot of time here," said Tim. "This is my home, the place where I spent my life!" Tim felt a cold chill spread over him. "Do you mean you're dead, that you are a ghost?" "Don't be afraid," said Vortan. "I'm your friend, I don't want to hurt you, just allow me to explain what has happened!"

Tim was petrified and didn't really have a lot of choice in the matter. Anyway, his legs felt like jelly, and he couldn't run, so he sat back down on the log. "OK!" said Tim, "go on, explain". Vortan reached over and took the metal object that Tim had found and held it out in front of him. "This is my sacred Axe, and when I was dying from my wounds hear in this wood, I struggled back to my hiding place right under where you're sat, it was my secret place where nobody should ever find me and steel my spirit. Before I died, I entrusted my spirit into my axe."

"My father who had been a great warrior before me gave me the axe." "My mother who was the spiritual leader of our tribe, she was a priestess, blessed and purified the axe on the altar of the gods, and when I was gone my spirit was locked into my axe and has remained there until now." "I have been waiting for you to come and release me!" Tim, stared at Vortan intently, he was very confused. "When you said, you have been waiting for me to come and release you, what did you mean by that?" asked Tim. "I have been drawing you hear for some time now, so you would eventually find the axe and release me!" said Vortan. Tim was even more confused at this remark. "How have you been drawing me hear?" "What do you mean by that?" Tim said. "Don't be alarmed," said Vortan, "I have always been a part of you, since you were born, a small part of my spirit joined you at your birth." "But it needed you to come and find the axe and release my spirit completely, in order to bring us together and make us one!" Timothy shook his head and rubbed his eyes to make sure he wasn't dreaming all this.

After reassuring himself it was actually happening, he looked at Vortan and said, "What do you mean make us one?" Vortan hesitated and looked long and hard at Timothy, and replied, "We are one, I am you, you are me, you are Vortan!" Tim felt his stomach turn over, he was feeling faint, he couldn't take all this in, it was just too much. Vortan stepped closer and gently placed his hand on Tim's shoulder to reassure him. "Don't be alarmed, I haven't come to hurt you, it is simply our destiny!" said Vortan. "I have been reincarnated in you!"

Timothy looked at Vortan, still very confused and asked, "Why are you covered in those wild colours, and why is your hair stood up like that, with that white stuff on it?" Vortan laughed and declared "I'm a warrior, this is what warriors look like!" "Well, you certainly look scary, I can understand that." "How long have you been dead?" Asked Tim. "I don't know really; many centuries!" replied Vortan. "Are you just known as Vortan, or do you have a second name?" asked Tim. Vortan laughed and hesitated. Then he said, "You might not want to know my other name." "Why not?" said Tim, quizzically? "I am called Vortan the Slayer!" said Vortan, and laughed again, loudly. Tim cringed; he was horrified. "You mean you have killed people?" Said Tim. "Of course!" said Vortan. "If you don't kill them, they will kill you!" "How many have you killed?" Asked Tim nervously. "I'm not sure," said Vortan, "more than fifty; they did call me the slayer you know!" "It sounds as if you liked killing people!" Said Tim accusingly. "It's a lot better than being killed," laughed Vortan. "As a warrior, you either kill or are killed!" "Anyway, I died trying to protect my family and my tribe from raiders from the Northern hills, they'd been trying to steal our homeland for a long time, and we had killed many of their warriors defending against them!" "We had lost many fine warriors also, but that's what life was like in those distant times!" "Very violent!" said Vortan sadly. Timothy was beginning to relax a little but was still very confused and had a thousand questions to ask. "Did you wear that paint and stuff all the time?" said Tim, "No!" laughed Vortan, "Close your eyes for a moment." Tim did as he was told and closed his eyes. Just a few seconds later Vortan said, "is that better for you then?" Tim opened his eyes and was amazed to see Vortan, stood there, all the paint gone, all the white substance gone out of his hair. He couldn't believe the transformation. Vortan was stood there, well over six feet tall, sun tanned, muscles rippling all over his body, blonde hair down past his shoulders, a blonde moustache hanging down his chin. He also had a heavy gold torque around his neck and wide golden armlets around his upper arms. He was also wearing some kind of pants this time, made from animal skin of some kind. Tim stared at him in amazement, Vortan looked like a Greek god Tim thought. "You look fantastic!" said Tim. Vortan laughed, "not so scary, like this then?" he said. "No," said Tim, "but you do look fit and strong!" "Well, I was considered to be the greatest warrior of my time you know," said Vortan. "But this is how I looked when I wasn't preparing for war!" He said with a smile. "Well, what now?" said Tim. Vortan looked at Tim Thoughtfully. "Don't be afraid, but it's time for you and me to become one!" "How do we do that?" said Tim. "Just close your eyes and relax!" Said Vortan, "We're meant to be together anyway!" Then Tim felt the strangest surge come over him, he opened his eyes and looked around, he felt different, stronger, more alert, his senses felt stronger. Then he realised Vortan was no longer stood in front of him. He looked around again and shouted, "Where are you?" Then came the reply, "I'm here, inside you!" "We are now one!" "We are now Vortan, and Tim!" "We are now complete!" "My spirit is now your spirit!" "My long sleep is over, thank you Tim!" Timothy felt strange and very confused, but he did feel extremely alert and much stronger than he ever felt before. He was beginning to accept Vortan's words.

"Tell me about your mother," said Tim "you said she was a priestess!" "Yes, she was very special", said Vortan, she was a druid her name was Merva, and when I was just a child she bestowed upon me, some special powers." "What kind of powers?" asked Tim, "Well the first thing is that I have extra strength and energy," said Vortan, "then I have the ability to read peoples thoughts," "I can also project my astral body to anywhere I want." "What does that mean?" said Tim. "Well, your astral body is a finer form of your physical body, it's what you saw earlier when you first saw me; sometimes called a ghost!" explained Vortan. "There are other things, but I'll explain them later!" "I know it's a lot for you to take in all at once, but we can work together, and I'll try and help you to understand!" said Vortan. "OK," said Tim, "but I must make my way home now, I'm very late, and I dread to think what my parents will say, especially my stepfather, I hope he hasn't been drinking again."

CHAPTER TWO

COMING HOME

Tim picked up his tools and the bronze axe head and put them in his shoulder bag, then taking his metal detector, set out for home. He ran across the fields towards his house on the edge of town, trying to make sense of everything that had happened in the last few hours, and trying to come to terms with his newfound strength and energy. He couldn't help jumping and skipping as he ran. He felt as if he could run for- ever, and he also felt like he could jump over houses, which was a lot different from before, when he suffered from asthma, and really felt quite weak and not very sporty. As he approached his house Tim started to feel a powerful sense of trouble.

He opened the back gate and saw his mother (Tina) stood at the back door. She was crying and her face was bruised. He'd been drinking again. Tim thought. "Where have you been until now? It's nine O' clock, you should have been home four hours ago!" said his mum. Tim tried to explain what had happened, but before he could say anything, his stepfather (Duncan) burst out of the back door, knocking his mother flying. "What have I told you about staying out till this time, you little swine!" Tim's stepfather, shouted as he stormed across the yard with his right fist raised above his shoulder, as he'd done many times before. This time, Tim didn't cower, as he'd done in the past. Instead, he stepped forward and hit Duncan in the middle of his chest, with the heel of his left hand, causing Duncan's feet to fly in the air and sending him crashing to the floor flat on his back. He didn't move. He was stunned. Tim stepped forward again, leaned over him and hit him with his right fist full in the nose. Duncan groaned and closed his eyes, as the blood started running from his nostrils. "Tim", his mother shouted, "what are you doing?" "No more" said Tim, "we're not putting up with any more of his brutality!" "Look at the state of him!" said Tim's mum, "what are we going to do with him, what about when he wakes up." "Don't worry," said Tim, "everything will be alright." Then Tim went into the kitchen and came out with a jug of water. He walked over to Duncan who was still unconscious on the floor. He threw the contents of the jug straight into Duncan's face. "Ah" Duncan groaned as he recovered consciousness, "where am I? What happened?" Tim reached down and took hold of Duncan's throat, and squeezed, and as Duncan gasped for breath. Tim said "any more violence from you and I'll kill you! Do you understand?" Duncan who was in no position to disagree at that particular time nodded his head and Tim let go of his neck.

Tim's mum was completely dumbstruck, she couldn't understand the complete transformation in Tim. He had always been so timid. He wouldn't fight with anybody before, he wouldn't even stand up for himself with the girls in his school, that's why they called him timid Tim.

Her Timothy had changed into a completely different character. He seemed bigger, stronger, and full of confidence and the fearless aggression was a complete mystery to her; even his voice had changed. "Timothy, I need to talk to you, right now, come in the house this minute!" She spoke. Tim followed his mum into the house. "Now tell me, what is going on with you?" Timothy heard Vortan's voice in his head. "She'll never believe you!" he said. "Tell me, what possessed you to behave like that, and where did you learn to fight that way all of a sudden?" "You wouldn't believe me if I told you!" Said Tim, apologetically. Just then Duncan staggered into the kitchen from the yard. "My nose is broken," he said. Tim turned towards him and stared at him with piercing eyes, Duncan took a step back. "Don't hit me again, please," he pleaded. "Sit down here." Tim said, pointing to the chair at the end of the kitchen table. "What are you going to do?" asked Duncan nervously. "Fix it", said Tim, "hold on to the arms of the chair". Then without any hesitation Tim put one hand on Duncan's head and with the other took hold of the (out of shape) nose and very quickly snapped it back into place before Duncan had chance to object. "There you are," said Tim. "Now behave yourself in future, or it will be a lot more than your nose that will need fixing." Tim's mother stood watching all this with her mouth open completely dumbfounded. "Where did you learn to do that?" She said, "What's happened to you?" Timothy looked thoughtfully at his mother, "can I please explain tomorrow, I'm very tired, and I have school in the morning, it's Monday, and I don't want to be late." Tim went up to his room, taking his shoulder bag with him. He wasn't really tired, he was buzzing with energy, but he couldn't attempt to explain what had happened in front of his step- father, although Duncan probably would have believed anything, at 'that,' particular moment in time, he was so bewildered.

Tim sat on his bed, deep in thought, wondering how he was going to cope with all this change. He felt like a completely different person. He loved his mother and didn't know how he was going to explain why and how he had come to change like he had. "Tell her the truth!" Came the voice in his head (it was Vortan) "and if she doesn't believe you, at least you have been honest, and tried." "Ok," said Tim, "I'll try, but I don't hold out much hope." "Anyway, I need to look for something in my books". He rummaged through his bookshelf until he found the book he wanted. It was a book on archaeology, and Tim flicked through the pages until he came to a page filled with pictures of axe-heads, of different shapes, and different metals. As he put his finger on the picture of the axe-head he had found, and read the caption next to it, he fell back on the bed and stared into space. Vortan spoke, "what is it?" "Well, if you can read thoughts, you should know," said Tim. "I know what you're thinking, but I don't know why you're upset," said Vortan. "I'm upset because it says here that your axe is more than Two and a half thousand years old," said Tim. "Oh that: well, I did tell you I had been waiting a long time, didn't I", said Vortan. "Actually, two thousand seven hundred years," said Tim. "That's not a long time; that's forever!" Vortan laughed, well it's not you that's been stuck there all that time it's me, so don't be so upset, I'm free now, thanks to you, so let's be happy and get on with it, shall we?"

CHAPTER THREE

VORTAN'S LIFE

Tim's favourite subject at school was history and he was eager to learn more about Vortan and his life. If Vortan was a warrior, Tim thought, and lived around hear Two thousand seven hundred years ago, he was a 'Celtic Warrior." "Tell me all about yourself and your life." Tim said to Vortan, "I want to know everything!" Vortan laughed, "Everything," he said quizzically: "I don't think so". "Why not?" said Tim. "Because there are some things about my life then that you would find very hard to understand: violent and bloodthirsty!" Tim thought for a moment, then said to Vortan, "I've been having strange dreams since I was very young. Dreams about battles, with lots of shouting and fighting more like nightmares really." "They're probably my memories coming through to you!" Said Vortan sadly. "It was a very violent time, and my tribe was under constant attack from a particular tribe from the northern hills, 'The Cunai', they were determined to steal our land because it was a beautiful and fruitful place to live". "We had many battles with them and killed many of their warriors!" "But in the end: I died fighting them off, along with all my family and what was left of my tribe!" There was a long silence. "What about your family," said Tim? "Tell me about your family". Vortan hesitated, he was obviously distressed, thinking about his family, and what had happened to them all those years ago. To him it was like yesterday. After a while he spoke. "I had a beautiful wife, Mowena, and two sons, Conary, and Daylan, they were just infants, two and four: they were all slaughtered in the last battle." He hesitated again, and then spoke. "My mother who was Merva, the high priestess of our tribe, also perished there that day, but not before putting powerful curses on The Cunai!" "She decreed that 'any Cunai trying to live on our land would become infertile and eventually die childless', so they didn't last in that place for very long!" "What about your father?" asked Tim? "He was already dead," replied Vortan, "he had died fighting in the service of his farther (King Erin) of the Eastern Kingdom, some years earlier". Tim lowered his head in thought. "You had a difficult life, Vortan." Said Tim. "Yes." Said Vortan, "but I was lucky, I had a good family who cared for me, just like your mother cares for you." Tim was very thoughtful, "time to sleep now; we'll talk some more tomorrow." "OK," said Vortan, "but if you have strange dreams tonight, don't be afraid: it will just be my memories coming through to you, and I will explain them tomorrow for you!" Tim dreamed the night away. A thousand pictures flashing through his mind, mostly incomprehensible.

When he awoke in the morning he lay there wondering if the whole thing had been a ridiculous dream, but then the voice in his head started, "hi Tim, how do you feel today after a good sleep". It was Vortan. It wasn't all a dream; it had really happened. Tim lay there for a few minutes trying to make sense of it all. It was incredibly early, barely dawn. "Well,", said Tim, "Tell me about your life. Vortan hesitated, and then spoke. "I was born around here, or at least where you found me, it was called 'Terravan', and it was a beautiful place to live." "We had many cattle, pigs and sheep, and the forest held many deer and wild boar." "We had also cleared land for crops of grain, which was plentiful. There were fruit trees and berries, freshwater steams, plus a deep spring well, with healing waters." "We were very happy there, apart from the continuous raiding by the Cunai tribe, who were jealous of our bountiful homeland." "The Cunai lived in the northern hills and their land was poor and barren. They were harsh and ugly people, who would rather steel than work or cultivate." "The Cunai were small ugly people with dark curly hair; most unpleasant." "Their warriors were no real match for our warriors; they were small and untrained compared with our much bigger, stronger and highly trained warriors." "When I was about your age, I was sent to the warrior school of the great Myogg, she lived in the Southwest Mountains, I think you call it Wales." "Myogg was related to my mother, and she was a fearsome warrior and practised strange magic." "I stayed with Myogg for three years and learned all the skills and trickery of her style of fighting, along with some of her strange magic." "Myogg was not someone you would want for an enemy; she was feared throughout the land." "I learned how to use a spear, a sword, a bow, and my favourite, the axe; also, I had to learn to fight without any weapons." "Myogg was particularly fond of this art, she could kill a man, or an animal in seconds with her bare hands, and not even leave a mark."

"She was a fearful woman! Large, strong and very fit and agile, and when she went into battle, she roared and screamed like a wild animal." "She frightened her own warriors as much as she frightened the enemy." "She was though, the greatest teacher of warriors in the land, but she was also very choosy about whom she would allow into her school; I was one of only six while I was there." "She was a wonderful person, and a very strong influence in my life!"

"When I returned home there was a great celebration held in my honour, when I was accepted as a warrior, and into manhood." "My father 'Etain' presented me with the axe that you found: it was in better condition then, and my mother blessed it on the sacred altar, in the very wood where you found it." "My mother presented me with a beautiful spear with a bronze head, plus a new hunting bow." My grandfather 'King Erin', had travelled from his kingdom in the east, and he presented me with the most beautiful gifts: a sword with a bronze blade and a golden handle, with precious stones, blue and red, embedded into the handle and hilt." "He also gave me a golden torque for my neck and golden armlets, also with precious stones set into them." "It was a very exiting day for me, one I shall never forget." Timothy found all this very interesting and most of all he was curious about the culture that Vortan was describing. He thought that people of that time, were far less sophisticated and cultured than this.

He spoke to Vortan. "Tell me something Vortan, if your warriors were so much more superior to the Cunai warriors, how was it that they managed to wipe out your tribe like they did?" Vortan paused for a moment before he answered. Then with sadness in his voice, he spoke. "We were betrayed by one of our own people!" "Most of our best warriors were off fighting for my grandfather, King Erin, in the east, against a large army from the north." "We had in our tribe, a man called 'Zophrick' who had ambitions of power, a man who thought he should have been made chief of our tribe when my father died, but my mother would not allow it saying that Zophrick was not a true member of our tribe." "He had been adopted and was not born of any family in the tribe." "Privately my mother said he was not to be trusted." "She could look into his mind, and she saw something evil there." "Anyway, it had already been decided by my father, that I would succeed him when he died, which is what actually happened." "Much to the anger of Zophrick. At the time of our last battle, Zophrick had been off on a so-called hunting expedition with his two sons, Vikwell and Balick." "I had told him we needed all our warriors at the time to defend our settlement as so many were off fighting for King Erin, but he insisted that there was cattle missing and someone had to go and find them and bring them back." "I didn't believe him, I knew he was lying, but he left in the night with his sons." "Four days later we were attacked at dawn by a Massive Cunai force; we had no chance of fighting off such a force with just a few dozen warriors." "When I was dying in my hiding place, I over-heard Cunai leaders saying they had Zophrick to thank for his information, and they most reward him." "They did; they killed him and his two sons, which is just what I would expect of the Cunai." "It was a black day for my tribe, the 'Vanai'!"

"For my part, I was struck by an arrow in the heart, I felt my life force draining away and struggled back to my hiding place; the place where you found me." It was necessary for me to hide, in order to stop the Cunai warriors from cutting off my head and stealing my spirit, so they could strengthen their own spirit." "As a precaution, I entrusted my spirit into my favourite weapon: my sacred axe." "I did manage to release at least a dozen or so Cunai warriors from their earthly toil, before I eventually succumbed, and left another six or seven with something to remember me by." "You mean you killed a dozen of their warriors before you died, said Tim." "Yes," said Vortan "that's what I mean." Timothy thought for a while then spoke. "It's all extremely violent and tragic, isn't it, to die like that?" "That is the destiny of a warrior," said Vortan, "not many warriors die of old age!" "The life of a warrior is a noble life: exciting, very much respected by those around you, but for most warriors, a short life." Timothy spoke, "I must explain something to you Vortan, before we go any further." "We are not allowed to go around killing people in this age, it is called murder, and murderers are locked away for many years, so you need to understand, you mustn't kill people, do you understand?" "I understand", said Vortan.

CHAPTER FOUR

EXPLAINING TO MOTHER

"I most get up now and face my mother," Tim said nervously. "How am I going to make her understand what has happened, she'll never believe me, she'll think I've completely lost the plot." "Just tell her the truth," said Vortan, "and if she doesn't believe you, it's not your fault is it." "Don't worry." Said Vortan, "we're together now, and whatever life throws at us, we will face together." Tim quickly showered and dressed and went downstairs. His mother was sat in the kitchen waiting for him, with tea and toast ready for breakfast. "Eat your breakfast Timothy, and then: explain to me what is going on with you." She said. "The way you behaved last night was so much out of character, it was as if it was somebody else altogether." Timothy looked at his mother, whom he loved dearly. He paused, and then spoke. "You're never going to believe me mother." "Try me." She said. Timothy explained exactly what had happened, from when he found Vortan's axe, and that Vortan was now part of him, and that he 'Timothy',

18

had always been part of Vortan since he was born. Tim expected his mother to burst out laughing, or simply ridicule him for talking such rubbish. He was so surprised when his mother looked at him with a strange expression and then went ahead to describe Vortan in perfect detail. "How did you know about Vortan?" Said Tim, "What's going on here?" "I have had dreams about him since you were born, but I didn't understand what they meant." "Now, all those dreams make sense." Said Tim's mother. "So, you believe me then?" said Tim. "Yes, I believe you, but do you think I could see this Vortan for myself?" Tim thought for moment then turned his mind inward and spoke to Vortan. "What do you think, can you oblige my mother with an appearance?" "Why not?" Said Vortan, "she has seen me many times before." With that Vortan appeared at the end of the dining table, opposite Tim's mum, in all his finery: gold torque and armlets, arms folded across his chest, hair clean and shining, down past his shoulders, he was smiling. Tina looked long and thoughtfully at Vortan. "Does he speak?" she said to Tim. "He does" said Tim, "but I don't think you will understand a word he says, it's a very strange language, and I couldn't make any sense of it." "He communicates with me through thoughts, direct to my mind." "Well" said Tim's mum, "Vortan's presence within you would explain the massive transformation of your behaviour last night, I knew it wasn't just my Tim doing that to Duncan." "Timothy explained that Vortan was a highly trained Celtic warrior with extra magical powers, such as being able read people's thoughts, and to transport his astral body anywhere he wishes." At that that moment Vortan disappeared. "What happened? Where has he gone?" Said Tina. "He's back with me," said Tim. "You must feel very strange with Vortan joining up with you." Tina said. "I do," said Tim, "but I'll probably get used to it eventually." "Anyway, it's time you got ready for school now," said Tina. "OK," said Tim. "You know," said Tina, "That if you go around telling people about this, they will just laugh at you and think that you have lost your mind." "I know that mother, don't worry I have no intention of telling anyone." "I agree with you, people would just think that I had lost it, so I'm not going to say anything to anyone." "Good," said Tina.

CHAPTER FIVE

BACK TO SCHOOL

Tim set off for school, dreading the usual confrontation with the bullies. He caught the bus on the main road for the two- mile trip downtown to school. He met his friend Sam on the bus. It was the first day back after summer holidays, and Tim wasn't looking forward to it. Sam and Tim were not that close, they were in the same class and unfortunately, they suffered the same kind bullying and humiliation at the hands of the school thugs. Tim wasn't very big for his age, but Sam was even smaller and quite skinny, which made him a soft target. While Tim and Sam had this affinity at school they didn't knock about much outside of school. They were both rather quiet and withdrawn. Chatting to Sam, he told him he'd spent a very interesting day on Sunday in Tarbock Woods with his metal detector. He was telling him how he'd found a Two and a half thousand-year-old bronze axe, when the bus stopped again. Tim stopped talking, he looked nervously to the front of the bus, where more people were getting on.

"Oh no!" said Tim, "Here's Bull-Iggy," "Don't look at him," said Sam. But it didn't make any difference. Stood in the isle of the bus next to Tim was a very large sixteen-year-old youth, glaring at Tim, his real name was John Higgins, and he was the captain of the rugby team. Bull-Iggy was six feet tall and about fourteen stone. He got away with a lot because he was so good at rugby. "How much have you got Timid?" The large youth growled. "I've just got my dinner money, leave me alone," said Tim. "Give it me," said Bull-Iggy, "Now, or I'll rip you're ears off." Tim put his hand into his pocket, but then paused, as he heard the voice in his head. It was Vortan. "Leave this to me Tim."

Bull-Iggy reached out to grab hold of Tim's right ear, but he didn't quite make it. Tim took hold of the bully's right wrist and rose out of his seat, as he turned towards him, he pulled him towards himself and butted him on the side of the head. Bull-Iggy hit the floor of the bus with a crash. He stayed there for a while, and then started to wake up with a painful groan. He pulled himself up to his feet and looked around in a daze, wondering what had happened to him. Then he focussed on Tim, who had by then sat back down on his seat. The rest of the passengers on the bus, who were mostly from Tim's school, looked on in amazement. They had witnessed Bull-Iggy performing many times before and no one was ever prepared to stand up to him, 'until now'. Tim stood up again, took hold of the bully, spun him round and slammed him down in his own seat next to Sam, patted him on the head and smiled at him. "Don't move," Tim said, you might hurt yourself again." Sam looked up at Tim, shook his head in amazement, then squeezed himself into the corner away from bull-Iggy, as he began to grasp what had just happened.

The bus stopped; it was time to get off. Tim helped Bull-Iggy off the bus, holding his arm, while the other kids looked on bewildered. When they reached the pavement Tim leaned towards Bull-Iggy and spoke in his ear. "Put your hands on me again and I will hurt you badly." With that Tim let go of his arm. Bull-Iggy staggered for a few yards then sat on a low wall, he wasn't feeling very well. He threw-up on the pavement, and his legs felt like jelly. He sat there for a while trying to take in what had just happened.

Tim and Sam set off up the road, just a short distance to their school. Sam, turned to Tim, he was very confused. "What's going on, do you realise what you've just done?" "We'll have to emigrate!" he said. "Don't worry," said Tim, "we'll be alright, but we're not taking any more thuggery off Bull-Iggy and his gang!" "Oh really!" Said Sam, "and how do you suggest we deal with them?" "We'll sort them out", said Tim. Sam looked at Tim and burst out laughing. "I hope we have a nice funeral," said Sam, mocking. Tim laughed and put his arm round Sam's shoulder. "Come on, let's enjoy the day, don't worry about that gang of thugs, we'll see to them later." Sam shook his head in disbelief as he thought to himself, this isn't Tim, it's a doppelganger, either that or, Tim's had a brainstorm, we're both going to be butchered.

When Tim and Sam got to their class, they became aware that the rest of the class was talking about what had happened on the bus. Timid Tim had flattened the school bully and didn't even seem to be that bothered about it at all. He was the only topic of conversation in the class. Timid Tim and his mate Sam had been the subject of many jokes played in the past two years, since starting at St Joe's. So, the question was. How did Timid Timothy Henderson manage to beat up Bull-Iggy, the biggest thug, not only in the school, but also in the town? The school was buzzing with the strange story. Sam was very concerned about what was going to happen at break-time. Bull-Iggy had a rather nasty gang, the prospect of mixing with them in the schoolyard wasn't a very appealing one. "Perhaps we could sneak out the back way and give the rest of the day a miss," suggested Sam to Tim. "Don't worry," said Tim, "we'll be alright, just stick together and we'll be fine." Sam thought for a moment, then looked straight at Tim and said, "but Tim I can't fight!" Tim put his hand on Sam's shoulder and said, "listen, just do this for me and we'll be OK, if anyone attacks me from behind just jump on their back and make a nuisance of yourself and leave the rest to me." "Do you think you could do that?" It was of course, not just Tim, but mostly Vortan that was talking. "I'll try," said Sam.

After morning lessons, they went to the dining hall for lunch, once again the two lads found themselves the subject of a great deal of talking and staring. Lunch finished, Tim and Sam went out into the schoolyard. It wasn't long before they were faced by the Iggy- gang, five of them, Bull-Iggy in the centre. Tim's thoughts turned inward to Vortan, "don't desert me now he thought." "Don't worry," replied Vortan, "we're together now, I won't let you down, just come along for the ride," Sam moved behind Tim nervously, wondering how he'd got into this situation. Bull-Iggy spoke, "What about it then Timid, you thought you were clever this morning didn't you?" Tim stepped forward and smiled but didn't speak. The bully couldn't figure out whether Tim was smiling or growling. The fact that he'd stepped forward instead of backwards confused him. By this time, a large crowed of boys and girls had gathered around in anticipation. The bully gang were urging their leader on, he was aware of the crowd, and conscious of his reputation. He was also aware that there was something strange about Timid Tim, he was indeed no longer timid, and he was smiling and appeared uncharacteristically very confident. It was very unnerving, but he couldn't back down now, not with this entire crowd watching, plus he had his gang behind him now.

Bull-Iggy lunged at Tim with his right fist. It was the signal for the game to begin. Tim stepped to the side and let out a loud yell as he punched Iggy in the right side of his body crunching his ribs. Bull-Iggy hit the floor with a thud, and as the rest of the gang piled in. Tim started yelling and screaming like a wild animal as he punched kicked and butted his way through the gang. One managed to run away, but the rest were on the floor groaning in pain. Two were unconscious, the other two were in a mess with blood running from their noses, mouths or eyes. The crowd was cheering wildly. Sam looked at Tim in amazement. Tim had a split lip and a gash over his left eye. He turned to Sam and smiled, he them looked at Bull-Iggy, lying on his back on the floor groaning. Instead of stepping over him, Tim stepped on Iggy's chest, who let out a loud groan, as he moved to Sam and put his arm around his shoulder. "Thanks mate," Tim said to Sam. "What for? I didn't do anything." "Yes, you did, you stood you're ground and didn't run off, that was worth a lot; you were very courageous." Sam smiled and pushed his chest out with pride. He had been called many things in his life, but never courageous. The crowd cheered and opened to allow Tim and Sam through "This is a very strange day," said Sam.

Tim and Sam were now heroes in the eyes of all their classmates, and the school bullies had been put in their place in no uncertain terms. Vortan spoke to Tim, "Well Tim, how does it feel being a Vanai warrior?" Tim laughed, "I've never felt so exhilarated in my life," but I think I have a few injuries, though I don't feel any pain." "Don't worry about the injuries, all warrior's get them, they'll soon heal," said Vortan.

After lunch Tim's teacher (Mr Conway) called him to the front of the class and asked him what had been going on in the playground. Tim explained that he'd been attacked by Bull-Iggy and his gang and was forced to defend himself. "Defend yourself," said Mr Conway; mocking, "There are four of them on their way to hospital." Timothy looked at Mr Conway, paused for a moment then spoke, "Tell me, what should I have done when they attacked me?" "I don't know," said Mr Conway, "But the headmaster wishes to speak to you, so go to his office right now." Tim looked at Sam shrugged his shoulders and smiled as he strode off down the corridor.

"Come in boy," the headmaster (Mr Whitfield) shouted." Tim stepped inside and stood in front of the desk, the headmaster looked at Tim and stared for a moment. "What's going on boy?" he said sternly, "there are four boys in an ambulance on their way to hospital, and I would like to know how they got in that state, so come on explain yourself." "They attacked me sir, so I had to defend myself." "You had to defend yourself?" "Yes Sir," said Tim. The headmaster stood up from his seat and walked round the desk and stood in front of Tim. He was about six feet tall, and he was towering over Tim. "You mean you took on four sixteen-year-olds and put them in hospital boy?" "No

Sir; there was five of them, but one ran off." said Tim. The headmaster looked puzzled. "There's going to be big trouble when their parents find out, you could be prosecuted you know." Tim stared at the headmaster for a moment. "You don't seem very concerned about my injuries, and as far as being prosecuted is concerned, I think that would be better than allowing that bunch of thugs to beat me up and put me in hospital wouldn't it Sir?" said Tim. "Listen to me boy, I will not permit this kind of behaviour in my school, do you understand that," said the headmaster. Tim thought for a moment then spoke. "Tell me sir if you won't put up with this kind of behaviour. How is it that Bull-Iggy, and his gang of thugs have been allowed to bully me and others, and steel our money ever since I started at this school, two year ago, and nobody has done anything to stop them?" The headmaster looked very sternly at Timothy, then retorted, "You're insolent boy! And I'm suspending you until this matter has been sorted out with your parents. Now get out of my office and go home."

Tim left the headmaster's office and was about to go and collect his bag from his classroom when Vortan spoke to him. "We most go home, right now Tim," There's trouble there." "What kind of trouble?" Asked Tim. "Trust me Tim, we must go right now," insisted Vortan. "I need to go and see the school nurse before I go home, and get these injuries dealt with," said Tim. "No, you don't," said Vortan, "I will sort that out as we go." "How will you do that," said Tim. "My mother was a great healer, and I was bestowed with the same powers when I was just a small child," said Vortan. "OK," said Tim, "but what sort of trouble at home, are you talking about?" "Mother," said Vortan, "and that drunken thug, Duncan." "Oh no!" said Tim, "not that again, we must hurry." Tim left his bag in class and ran straight down the corridor and out of the school, down the road to the bus stop, and caught the first bus home to Hough-Green. He jumped off the bus and ran straight home.

CHAPTER SIX

TROUBLE AT HOME

As Tim approached his house, he saw an ambulance outside. His Stomach turned as he thought about what could have happened. He dashed inside the house where he found two ambulance men putting his mother on a stretcher. She was unconscious. "What's happened?" Tim said to the paramedics, then he noticed the next-door neighbour, Mrs Kelly. "It was Duncan," she said, "he's drunk again." Tim went to look at his mother, he was horrified when he saw the condition she was in, her face bruised terribly, blood trickling from her nose, her lips swollen. She was almost unrecognisable. "Why is she unconscious?" Asked Tim. "She's had a knock on the head" said one of the paramedics, she probably knocked it on the floor when she fell." "I'm coming with her," said Tim. "OK, let's go," said the paramedic. Tim went in the ambulance with his mother to the hospital. On the journey to the hospital Tim held his mother's hand. He loved her so much and his thoughts were mixed. Worry; fury; anger. As the nurses took charge of his mother at the hospital and ushered Tim into a waiting room, he was terribly upset, he turned his thoughts to Vortan. "I'm frightened!" He said, "Mother might die!" "She's not that bad." Said Vortan, "she'll regain consciousness soon, but she needs to sleep now, it will help her to heal." "When she comes round, we will heal her wounds quickly." "How can you do that?" Asked Tim.

"Go and look in the mirror, at your injuries," said Vortan. Tim had been sat in the waiting room, then by his mother's bedside since the nurse had brought her to a side room, after being attended to by the doctor. He got up and went to the toilet, where he quickly went to look in the mirror. To his astonishment there wasn't a mark on his face. The gash over his left eye, and his bruised and split lip, had completely healed. He stared in amazement, touching and feeling his face with his fingers. "That's crazy," said Tim to Vortan. "That's healing," said Vortan. "And we will help mother later, but there is something I must do right now, alone." "Alone?" asked Tim, "but why?" "I'm going to leave you for a while, and I want you do something, and promise me you will stick to it." "What do you want me to do?" Asked Tim. "I want you to go back and sit with mother, and stay there until I come back, ask the nurse if you can stay there until mother comes round," said Vortan. "Where are you going?" quizzed Tim. "I have something to do and need you to stay here with mother." "Will you do that? Asked Vortan. "OK, but how long will you be?" asked Tim. "Not very long." said Vortan. Tim felt a strange sadness as Vortan left him. He'd got used to being together with Vortan and he liked the feeling very much. He went back to his mother's room and settled down for the night, in the chair at the side of her bed, and held her hand. The nurse smiled and put her hand on Tim's head, saying, "She'll be OK Tim."

Tim was still holding his mother's hand while resting his head on her bed, when he suddenly awoke with a start. It was Vortan returning. "How is mother now, Tim?" asked Vortan. "She's still unconscious as you can see," said Tim sadly. "I'm worried about her," he said. "What has the doctor said about her condition?" said Vortan. "They think she will be OK, but they don't know when she'll recover consciousness," said Tim. "Let's settle down for the night and see how she is in the morning," said Vortan. Tim put his head back down on the bed and closed his eyes.

Tim was awoken at 3. O clock in the morning by the nurse. "Somebody wishes to speak to you Tim, it's the police." "What do they want?" asked Tim. "I don't know but they are waiting in the office." The nurse took Tim to the Office, where there were two plain cloth's police officers waiting. Tim looked at them and asked what they wanted. "We've come to find out what has been going on with your family," said the taller policeman. "It took you long enough," said Tim, "my mother has been in a comer since 2. O clock yesterday afternoon, and you turn up now." The other policeman stepped forward and spoke. "It's not your mother we've come about, it's your father Duncan. "Have you arrested him?" snapped Tim, "he should be locked up for what he's done to mother, he's nothing but drunken thug!" The two policemen looked at Tim, quizzically. The taller one spoke. "Where have you been for the last few hours?" he said. Tim looked at him, with a disgusted look. "Where do you think I've been with my mother in this state? I've been here since my mother came in, I came in the ambulance with her, and I've been here ever since, Now leave me alone, and go and arrest that thug Duncan." The tall policeman asked the nurse if she could confirm that Tim had been there all that time, to which she answered, "of course I can he hasn't left her bedside except to go to the bathroom, since she came in yesterday, why are you asking?" The second policeman spoke, "Do you have any other relatives that can come and help?" Tim looked at them puzzled and said, "My grandfather is on his way, he should be here soon, why what's the problem?" he said. "We'll wait for him to come, said the taller policeman. Tim shrugged his shoulders and left the office and went back to his mother's room and sat by her bed.

CHAPTER SEVEN

DUNCAN

3.30 am, Tim was sat with his head on his mother's bed, he was fast asleep. He was woken up by his grandfather (Edgar), who put his hand on Tim's shoulder, "how are you bearing up son, you've had a lot to put up with haven't you?" "I'm alright granddad, its mother I'm concerned about," said Tim. "I don't want that thug Duncan in our house anymore."

"That's not going to be a problem!" said Edgar, "Duncan's dead!" Timothy looked very sternly at his granddad, "dead?" said Tim, "are you serious?" "I'm serious," said Edgar, that's why the police are here." "But how? And when?" said Tim. "Outside the pub, last night, about 11. 30!" said Edgar. "What happened?" said Tim. "Well," said Edgar, "the police don't really know! The story they got from Duncan's mates, is that when they came out of the pub, they walked just a few yards, when they met This weird looking character, which was covered in blue paint and had white hair all stuck up." "They said that they all started laughing at him, but when he began to growl like an animal, they started running instead." "When they looked round Duncan hadn't run at all, he was lying on the floor and the weirdo had disappeared!" "They went back to check on Duncan, but found that he wasn't breathing, it seems his neck was broken." "The police of course, don't believe this ridiculous story, they think that they were fighting amongst themselves, and made the story up in order to protect whoever did it!" Tim looked at his granddad with the strangest look. "What is it, Tim?" said his granddad. "Nothing!" said Tim. "I just want mother to get better!"

Tim turned his thoughts to Vortan, "I don't suppose you would know anything about Duncan's death would you, Vortan?" There was no reply, from Vortan. Tim spoke again, "Where did you go last night when you left?" This time Vortan replied, "I went back to the 'Nemeton'. "What's a Nemeton?" asked Tim. "The Nemeton is where you first found me," said Vortan, "it means 'sacred grove', our place of worship, the place we go to when we wish to speak with our gods, it was where I died, it was part of our place, our settlement." "You mean Tarbock Wood?" said Tim. "Yes," said Vortan, "that's what I mean." "Why did you go back there?" said Tim. "Because I needed to speak to the Gods!" replied Vortan. This was all a bit heavy for Tim, he didn't understand this talk of Gods, and sacred groves, but he thought he'd go along with it for now. "So, you went to talk to your gods, What about?" Vortan paused for a moment, then replied, "I needed to ask them for guidance about something you said to me." "What was that?" asked Tim. "Well you said, I was not to go round killing people, because things were different in this age, and that it was against the law, but I was confused because the law didn't seem to care about what happened to mother, and if Duncan was allowed to carry on doing what he was doing he would probably kill her soon!" "So, I asked the Gods for their guidance!" "And what did they say?" asked Tim. "They told me to follow my conscience, so I did!" "You mean you killed him?" "Yes," said Vortan. "I didn't want him dead, I just wanted him to leave us alone!" said Tim. "He was not going to leave you alone and you know that don't you Tim." "I could read his thoughts, and he had no intention of changing his ways, he would carry on until he killed either you or your mother or both!" declared Vortan. "Anyway, he's dead now, so let's get on with more important matters shall we." "Like what," said Tim. "Like waking mother up and helping her to recover from her injuries." Said Vortan.

CHAPTER EIGHT

WAKING MOTHER

"Mother is not asleep, she's in a comer!" said Tim, "you can't just wake her up." "Oh really?" said Vortan. "How would you like to go on a journey into your mother's mind?" said Vortan, and have a conversation with her, then you can reassure her and tell her to wake up?" "How can I do that?" asked Tim. "Just close your eyes and relax and let your mind join with mine." Tim found himself looking at his mother's thoughts: pictures of violence and confusion, running and calling out for help, but none coming. "Talk to her Tim," said Vortan, "tell her everything is going to be alright now, and that Duncan can't hurt her anymore, tell her it's time to wake up now." Tim did as Vortan suggested, and just then his mother started to blink her eyes. Within a few seconds Tina had her eyes wide open and was looking at Tim, and her father Edgar. Tim felt a warm feeling of relief flow right over him. He turned his thoughts to Vortan and said silently, "Thank you Vortan." His mother looked at him and said, "I heard that Tim," then she smiled. Tim and his grandfather both laughed with delight as tears of joy ran down their faces. She was going to be all right. The nurse was delighted that Tina had recovered consciousness and brought the doctor to check her over. The doctor was delighted that Tina had recovered consciousness, he spoke to her for a few minutes as he checked her over, then turned to Tim, and Edgar, "I think the worst is over and she's going to be alright, he said, "It will take some time but she's on the mend now."

Edgar suggested that he and Tim could go home now and allow Tina to get some rest, they could return tomorrow after getting some sleep themselves, and cleaning the house up after all the trouble of yesterday. They didn't mention to Tina, that Duncan had been killed, she'd had enough to contend with for now, and Edgar asked the nurse not to allow anybody else to tell her, the nurse agreed. Tim and his granddad left and went home, it was 5.O clock in the morning, and they were both ready for a sleep.

It was almost noon the next day when Tim woke up. He turned to Vortan and asked for an explanation about yesterday, and especially, Duncan's death. "Would you prefer it if Duncan was alive and well, and able to do the same again?" said Vortan. "Anyway, that's in the past now and there's nothing anyone can do about it." "What's more important is that we help mother to recover, and forget about Duncan, he's not worthy of any consideration, he was a monster. "Perhaps he was," said Tim, "but we can't go round killing people like that!" "You didn't!" said Vortan, "I did! So, you can keep a clear conscience can't you." "It's against the law to kill people!" said Tim. Vortan thought for a moment then replied. "The law didn't do much to protect your mother, did it?" Tim couldn't deny Vortan's argument, but he wasn't happy with people being killed. "Let's concentrate on getting mother fit and well again, and making her life a happy one, shall we?" said Vortan. "I can't argue with that, said Tim, the first thing we need to do is clean up the house and make it good for when she comes home!"

Tim set about tidying up the house, it was in a mess with broken chairs and dishes all over the kitchen. He worked away for about two hours, when his grandfather came back from the hospital. "How's mother?" asked Tim. "She's still quite ill, but she's going to be alright eventually I think!" said Edgar. "Can I go and visit later?" said Tim. "Of course," said Edgar, "We'll finish cleaning this place up, and have some dinner, then we can spend the rest of the day at the hospital." "OK," said Tim, "but what about Duncan." "Forget about Duncan," said Edgar, "we're all better off without that thug, your mother wouldn't be in hospital if it wasn't for him." "I don't know what happened to him, but it's no more than he deserved," said Edgar. Tim heard Vortan saying something in his head. "I told you so," said Vortan. Tim looked thoughtful for a moment, trying not to reply to Vortan out loud. "I suppose the police will be coming back to talk to us soon." "Don't worry about them," said Edgar, let's concentrate on getting your mother fit and well again." "I told you so," said Vortan again, smugly. Tim was struggling not to tell Vortan to shut up in front of his granddad. "Let's finish the cleaning shall we," said Tim.

After cleaning the house making everything presentable, Tim and his granddad went to visit Tina in hospital. As they approached her bedside, they were amazed to see her sat up in bed, and looking very much improved, she was smiling and her bruises were almost gone, which was incredible after just twenty-four hours. Edgar looked at her and shook his head. "How have you recovered so quickly, it's amazing?" he said. Tina smiled and said, "I had a little help from Vortan, he sat here the whole night chanting prayers to some ancient gods!" "Who's Vortan?" asked Edgar. Tina looked at Tim and smiled again, then turned to her father, Edgar and said, "Tim will explain later, Vortan is a friend of the family now." Edgar looked at Tim quizzically. Tim looked at his mother, "I can't believe how well you look after yesterday, what has the doctor said?" "He said, I can go home in a couple of days if I continue improving like I have done up until now, he is very confused as to how I have made such a rapid recovery." "I told him that I had a little help from the gods, he just laughed." Edgar and Tim decided that it would be better if they didn't tell Tina about Duncan's death until she had recovered a little more, so they steered clear of any conversation concerning Duncan.

"How have you gone on at school?" Tina enquired. Tim though for a moment, not wanting to upset his mother unnecessarily, "They've given me some time off!" said Tim, as he glanced across the bed to his granddad. Edgar looked back at him quizzically. "How long have they given you?" said Edgar. "They didn't say!" replied Tim. "I'll stay off till mother is OK!" Tim and Edgar stayed for an hour, then made their way home, quite pleased with the progress Tina had made with her recovery.

CHAPTER NINE

EXPLAINING TO GRANDDAD

When they arrived back home Edgar looked at Tim sternly, "Who is Vortan?" he said. Tim was very hesitant; he didn't think his grandfather would ever believe his story. "He's a friend!" declared Tim. "Why have I never heard of him before now?" said Edgar, with an accusing tone in his voice. "Well," said Tim, "I've only recently met him." "Where does he come from?" Asked Edgar. "From around here," said Tim, trying to avoid the subject. "How old is he?" "I'm not sure," said Tim, realising he was being pushed into a difficult corner. "Come on Tim, is he your age, your mother's age, or my age, you must know roughly?" Tim looked at his granddad thoughtfully, realising he wasn't going to get out of this one easily. "Well roughly, Vortan is about two and a half thousand years old, I'm not sure exactly, neither is he!" Tim said finally. Edgar looked at Tim sternly. "You had better explain yourself young man, now." Tim could hear Vortan giggling inside his head as he set about telling his granddad his story about how he came to meet Vortan in Tarbock Wood. Edgar sat and listened patiently, but completely unconvinced until Tim had finished. "Do you really expect me to believe that ridiculous story?" he said, scoffing at Tim. "You have a very vivid imagination Tim, but that is a crazy story, and nobody would believe it!" Tim looked at his granddad once more and spoke. "Sit down granddad, please. He turned his thoughts to Vortan. "You're going to have to show yourself to granddad aren't you." "OK" said Vortan, and at once appeared in front of Edgar: war paint and all, clutching a long bronze headed spear in one hand and a gold handled bronze sword in the other. He looked fiercely at Edgar, then raised his sword and started speaking in a strange language. Edgar pushed back in his chair and gasped in amazement as he winced in fear, wondering what was coming next. "Don't worry," said Tim as he beckoned Vortan back. With that, Vortan disappeared once more, and Edgar sat up with his mouth wide open staring at Tim. "Well, do you believe me now?" said Tim, looking at his granddad. Edgar nodded his head but couldn't really speak. "That's Vortan!" said Tim, "and he is now part of me, he has apparently always been a part of me, but only a small part of him!" "The greater part of his spirit has been locked in his sacred, bronze axe since he was cut down in his last battle with his arch enemy, the Cunai!" "He says he has been waiting for me to come and release him by digging up the axe and cleaning it, which I did last Sunday!" Edgar eventually recovered from the shock of seeing Vortan in his war paint and struggled to speak. "Where is he now?" "He's inside me, I told you he is now a part of me, we are now one!" said Tim. Edgar thought for a while, trying to make some sense of all the strange things that had happened over the last few hours. He had a lot of questions but didn't know where to start.

CHAPTER TEN

IGGY'S REVENGE

After dinner Edgar was dosing in the chair when there was a knock at the door. Tim went to answer it but hesitated as the voice in his head cautioned him to be careful. He opened the door cautiously. There stood in front of him was a rather large angry looking man. "I want to speak to this 'thug Timothy' who beat up my son!" "Who are you?" Said Tim. "I'm Jack Higgins, and my son's in hospital, so where is he." The man demanded. Tim heard the voice in his head again. "Leave it to me Tim," Vortan said. "I'm Timothy, what do you want?" The man stared at Tim in disbelief. "You're not the one who beat up my son, where is he?" "I'm afraid it was me," said Tim. The man stared at Tim angry but confused, then reached out to grab hold of him with an exceptionally large right hand, snarling as he did so. But before he had chance to do or say anything else, he crumpled to the floor, letting out a deep groan after being hit in the solar plexus with the most savage blow from Tim with the outstretched fingers of his right hand. The commotion had awoken Tim's granddad and brought him rushing to the door.

"What's going on?" demanded Edgar, as he looked down at the large man, motionless on the ground outside the front door. "He grabbed me and was about to beat me up, so I had to stop him!" Declared Tim, looking down at the sorry sight of Bull-Iggy's father lying outstretched flat on his back, eyes wide open, not moving. "How did you do that?" demanded Edgar in disbelief. "Never mind that for now, if we don't revive him soon, we'll have a lot more explaining to do!" said Tim, but it was really Vortan talking. Edgar looked on in amazement his grandson stepped out, took hold of the man's shoulders and sat him up, then placed a knee in the middle of the man's back, took hold of his shoulders by placing his hands over the top of them. Then with an almighty yell, pulled back on the man's shoulders opening up his chest in a rapid action. Just then the man coughed and jumped to his feet with wild glaring eyes. Edgar stepped back in amazement. "How did you do that Tim?" he said. "It wasn't me; it was Vortan!" declared Tim. Just then Tim turned his attention to the big man who was by now, looking agitated and confused. Tim reached out with his left hand and placed it on the man's chest. The man stepped back nervously. Tim stared at the man fiercely, then he spoke in a very threatening voice, "Go home, and stay away from me, or you may not wake up next time, do you hear?" Tim stepped forward; the man was trembling as he stepped back. "Go," shouted Tim. "Now." The large man didn't look so large as he hurried away with his head down. Edgar looked at Tim and shook his head in disbelief as he stepped back into the house Tim followed. "That wasn't me granddad, it was Vortan!" said Tim. "I believe you Tim," said Edgar. "I'm quite sure that, on your own you would not be capable of such incredible violence, or the ability to revive somebody like you did." "Tell me something Tim," said Edgar, "was that man unconscious or was it worse than that?" Tim thought for a moment. "Well, he wasn't breathing, but he's OK now isn't he." Edgar shook his head. "You know you can't go round killing people like that don't you." "We didn't have much choice granddad, he attacked me, and he didn't come here to wish us well, he's a thug just like his son!" "You know his son then?" Said Edgar. "I know him well!" Said Tim, "he's been bullying me at school since I started at St Joseph's, taking my dinner money and anything else I had, and not just me but anybody he thought he could push around!" Edgar thought for a moment, "why didn't you say something to your mother about what was going on?" he said. "Mother has had enough to contend with recently," said Tim. "Anyway, I don't think he'll be bothering anybody for a while!" "Why is that?" said Edgar. "Well," said Tim, "when he tried bullying me on Monday, Vortan took over and put him and his gang in hospital, causing the headmaster to suspend me from school until further notice!" "I didn't tell mother because she had enough problems to be going on with!" "I see," said Edgar, "I'll go to the school and speak to the headmaster for you, I despise bullies!"

CHAPTER ELEVEN

TINA COMES HOME

Two days later Tim's mother (Tina) was released from hospital, the doctors and nurses were amazed at her remarkably quick recovery from such injuries. She smiled and thanked them all for their kindness and caring, and repeated that she had been helped by the Gods and of course, her family. The doctor smiled patronisingly, then said take it easy at home and thank your Gods for me, I wish we had their help more often, we would have a lot of empty beds in this place, he laughed. Edgar and Tim took Tina home. On the way she enquired about Duncan asking whether he'd been around causing any further trouble while she was in hospital. Tim steered the conversation away from Duncan by owning up to being suspended from school. Tina turned and gave Tim a stern look, "why have you been suspended from school?" she demanded. Edgar smiled as he drove, knowing how Tim had managed to distract her from the subject of Duncan. "I got into a disagreement with another boy and his friends, and the headmaster decided to suspend me until he had made some enquiries about what went on, I think he would like to speak to you when you're feeling stronger," said Tim. Tim's granddad Edgar intervened tactfully. "I will go and speak to him later today" he said, "let's just concentrate on getting you settled down." "OK," said Tina, but I want to know what he has to say." They arrived home and Tina was so pleased to see that the house was so clean and tidy. "You have been busy," she said as she settled on the couch and Tim brought a blanket from upstairs.

Next day Edgar set off for Tim's school to speak to the headmaster. Tina called Tim from the kitchen where he was washing the dishes after lunch. Come and sit down and talk to me. Tim came and sat down hesitantly, for he knew what was coming next. Tina looked at her son, took hold of his hand and squeezed. "Now tell me about Duncan, and don't try changing the subject again," she said firmly. Tim looked down, hardly knowing how to begin. Finally looking up he gathered himself and spoke. "Duncan is dead," he said hesitantly, "he died the night you went into hospital." "What happened?" said Tina, Her eyes wide open in surprise. "I hope you didn't have anything to do with it," she said. "I was in the hospital with you all night," said Tim. "The police think there was an altercation outside the pub with Duncan and his mates, and he ended up with a broken neck." Tim thought it would be a good idea not to mention the part of the story about the strange looking creature that frightened the gang into doing a runner. Tina lay back on the couch deep in thought. Tim couldn't decide whether his mother was relieved or saddened at the news of Duncan's death. Perhaps both, he thought.

Tim's granddad, (Edgar) knocked on the office door of the headmaster (Mr Whitfield), "come in" was the response. Edgar stepped inside, he was a quiet man in his late fifties, but he was not someone to be fooled about with and he commanded a great deal of attention when he was angry. And he was angry. He stared firmly at the headmaster, "why have you suspended my grandson from school, when he was the one who was assaulted by a gang of thugs, tell me that will you?" The headmaster shrank from a confrontation with Edgar, not so much because of the words, but because of the way they were delivered. He replied sheepishly. "Well, there are four boys in hospital, thanks to your grandson, and I have to do something to keep some discipline you know." Edgar stepped forward to the front of the headmaster's desk. "Discipline." He shouted as he slammed his hands down on the desk. "You don't know what discipline is, you miserable excuse for a man, you have allowed this Higgins boy and his gang of thugs to bully and rob children in this school for years!" Where's the discipline in that?" Edgar banged his hands down on the desk once again, this time with his fists clenched. The headmaster winced as he pushed his chair back from the desk. "I'm doing all I can, I can't watch them all the time." Spluttered the headmaster apologetically. Edgar stood up square and fixed his eyes firmly on the headmaster. "You sort this out or I will have a meeting with the governors and get you sorted out. I'll discuss all the thuggery you have allowed to go on in this school." The headmaster apologised to Edgar and suggested that Timothy could come back to school as soon as he was ready. Edgar nodded his head, turned and left the headmasters office.

Back at home Tim was sat with his mother, trying to comfort her after all she had gone through in the last few days, Tim was very close to his mother. He felt even more so now. "How do you feel now?" Tim asked. "I'm OK," Said Tina, thanks to you and granddad, and of course we mustn't forget your friend Vortan must we?" Tina smiled. Tim was relieved to see that she was smiling instead of scolding him about Vortan. "He was wonderful you know, when I felt really weak and miserable, he came and stayed with me all night, and prayed the whole time for his gods to give me strength and courage, and I have to say it really worked, because in the morning I felt so much better." She took hold of Tim's hand and squeezed. "You must thank him for me." She spoke. "Not necessary." said Tim, "he hears you." Tina smiled and lay back on the couch and closed her eyes.

CHAPTER TWELVE

VORTAN'S LIFE

Tim left his mother to have a sleep, he went to his bedroom and turned his thoughts to Vortan. "I want to know more about your life and your family," he said to Vortan. "The best way to find out about my life is to close your eyes and allow your mind to join with mine and share my memories while I cast my mind back to things that happened when I was growing up in our settlement," said Vortan. "OK," said Tim, "that sounds like a good idea, let's try it." Tim lay back on his bed closed his eyes and allowed his mind to join with Vortans's. He was amazed to find himself walking through thick forest in a line with other people, the man in front of him was a large fearsome looking warrior with war- paint on his body and white in his hair, the man was carrying a large spear in his right hand, a dagger in his left hand and a bronze sword hanging on his left side. Just then, the man in front crouched down as he reached the edge of the trees and undergrowth, he found himself and the rest of the band following suit and crouching down in silence. Tim could see that in the clearing ahead of them was a group of men, (about a dozen) leading half a dozen cattle towards the opposite side of the clearing. They waited until the men and the cattle disappeared into the woods on the far side of the clearing. The large man in front of Tim turned and looked at him, Tim was horrified to see how fearsome he looked with piercing eyes and a scar that reached from below his left eye to his chin. His face was covered in blue stripes as was his body, he was almost naked apart from a kind of sash or belt, which held his sword and a hammer- like object. Tim was aware of the extraordinarily strong smell that emanated from these men, it was completely unlike anything he had ever met in his life before. The man spoke, but it was that same language that Vortan had used when he had first met him, the only word Tim understood was "Vortan." Just then the band of warriors that Tim was with separated into two groups. Vortan leading one group to the left, and the other man taking the other group to the right, travelling around the edge of the clearing. The group moved quickly and quietly through the undergrowth. Tim saw that most of his group were carrying spears, but there were also six bowmen. All of them had either swords or axes in their belts. Tim noticed that he, or to be more precise Vortan was carrying a spear and a beautiful bronze sword with a golden handle beset with precious stones, plus his sacred axe, as well as a bronze dagger, all but the spear was tucked into his belt.

After tracking round the edge of the clearing to the far side, they picked up the trail of the cattle and the other men. Following the trail of the cattle was easy as the undergrowth was flattened. Soon they could hear voices and the occasional sound of a cow mooing. Vortan turned to his group, nodded to them and gestured for them to hurry. As they came in sight of the cattle and the men the whole group started yelling and screaming as they ran towards them. The cattle bolted through the trees and the men quickly followed, they were all carrying spears. They were all obviously warriors, but they were vastly different from Vortan and his warriors. They were not so tall, and they all had jet black hair, and they didn't wear war-paint. As they ran, they abandoned the cattle which scattered in all directions. The men stayed together in one group running very fast down a path in the woods, when suddenly, they stopped dead in their tracks.

Tim noticed as Vortan and his group closed in on the men, just ahead of them, stood in a half circle was the other half of Vortan's warriors. The men looked terrified as they realised, they had been surrounded. Tim felt quite impressed when he thought how cleaver the trap had been set, but he was horrified when he saw what came next. The two groups of Vortan's tribe closed in on the outsiders screaming and shouting, they hacked them to death in minutes and finished by decapitating each of them and dancing round holding the outsider's heads by the hair. Tim felt sick as he saw this gruesome, barbaric sight. He had never imagined that things could be so cruel and bloodthirsty. Vortan and his men rounded up the cattle and headed back home, dancing and singing, and holding up the decapitated heads of the outsiders like trophies of war. Tim was horrified by the scenes he was witnessing, but he was determined to stick it out and find out more about Vortan and his life, no matter how gruesome it might be, he knew that he was witnessing Vortan's memories and that he was in no personal danger. Nevertheless, it was the most horrifying experience of his life, and he knew it wasn't just a dream. As they travelled through the woods Tim took the opportunity to study the warriors and how they behaved. He noticed they were all tall men, over six feet, except for the younger warriors, some of whom were no older than Tim himself, he was quite taken aback by the thought of going to war at his age, even more so by the thought of being slaughtered in battle. He tried to put that idea out of his mind, especially the thought of being decapitated, or having to do that to someone else.

Eventually the warriors arrived at a clearing and the large fearsome man who appeared to be in charge directed some of the men to take the cattle to their pen on the far side of the clearing. As they emerged from the trees a group of children set off across a small bridge over a deep ditch and ran towards the warriors shouting and waving. They hesitated when they saw the decapitated heads being held up by the jubilant warriors. Tim could see in the distance across the other side of the bridge, a large embankment about ten feet high with an opening like a gateway. There were plumes of smoke rising from the other side of the bank. As they approached the wooden bridge across the fast-flowing stream, Tim noticed just the other side of the bridge, were two poles stuck in the ground, one either side of the gateway. On top of which was a gruesome decomposing head. It seemed to act as a warning, either to keep out or enter at your peril. Either way it was very scary and certainly not very inviting. They passed through the gateway and into a large encampment with huts all around the outer edge and a much larger hut in the centre of the camp. The huts were round with sloping roofs and appeared to be made of straw and wooden branches with mud and straw for the walls.

As the warriors came into the encampment dancing and waving the enemies heads, all the women and children came out to greet them. Tim was surprised to see that, not only were the women and children not horrified by the sight of the decapitated heads, but they were cheering and dancing around the warriors, congratulating them on their success. It seems the outsiders had come the previous night and stolen their cattle. The large fearsome looking man who had been leading the warriors was apparently the tribal chief, Vortan's father. When he was in his own camp, he seemed much less fearsome, all the children crowding round him, fighting to get close to and touch him. Then without warning all the children ran off to one of the huts on the far side of the compound. Stood in front of the warriors was the tall figure of a woman, though most of the people in the settlement were almost naked, this woman was dressed in a long white robe that reached down to her ankles. She had jet black hair down to her waist, beautiful deep blue eyes that scanned the group meticulously. The whole group stood still in silence, including Vortan's father, the chief, as if waiting for her approval. She stared at each of the severed heads in turn, then turned to the chief and nodded, mumbled a few unrecognisable words turned and walked off to the largest hut in the centre of the settlement.

The warriors carrying the heads turned and left the compound, went back across the bridge and disappeared round to the left along the stream and into the woods carrying the severed heads with them.

The next picture Tim had was of a strange gathering in some woods at nighttime. There was a clearing, it was an eerie place, not just a natural clearing but one made purposely, circular, about fifty feet across. There were logs lying down in a circle, they had been trimmed, obviously for sitting on, they were all full of girls and women of all ages. Stood behind them all around the outside of the circle were at least two hundred warriors in war paint, all holding spears, the heads of which were glistening in the moonlight. There were half a dozen fires burning in a circle around the centre, were there was a sandstone slab resting on two sandstone pedestal slabs. The whole thing stood about three feet high and had some kind of torch soaked in oil burning on each end. The people were all quiet with anticipation, waiting for what? Tim thought. When in the distance, there was singing, growing louder as they drew nearer, female voices singing in a strange tongue. Then through an opening in the trees at the far side of the clearing, they appeared. The tall dark woman from earlier dressed in her white robe, but this time she was wearing a heavy gold torque around her neck and a crown of white flowers in her hair. She was a beautiful woman in her mid-thirties, she walked slowly, followed by twelve young girls carrying torches, all dressed in white robes, they were singing a gentle hymn-like song, dancing and swaying as they progressed. The girls were all barefoot and wore cords around their waists, they had crowns of flowers in their hair. Then as the girls entered the circle Tim heard a different kind of noise, it was men's voices, and they were chanting an eerie kind of song. Then they entered the circle. It was a gruesome sight. Twelve warriors in full war-paint, carrying spears in one hand, while in the other, they were holding the severed heads from their earlier encounter. They were holding the heads up high by the hair.

As they entered the circle, the whole assembly started cheering, while the spearmen at the outer part of the circle started shuffling and chanting along with the head carriers. Tim figured out that the Woman who led the proceedings was Vortan's mother, as he had told Tim that she was the tribal priestess. She was now stood in front of the stone slab, which looked very much like an altar. The girls had placed bowls and jugs on the slab then stepped back with their torches to form an open circle by the seated women and younger girls. Then, just when everyone was quietening down a lone figure entered the circle, and everyone cheered again. It was the leader of the war party from earlier. It was Vortan's father Etain. He still had his sword hanging on his belt, but he was wearing pants now and he was carrying a bowl with both hands which he placed on the slab in the centre, then he turned to the priestess, his wife Merva and nodded. Merva looked at the warriors with the heads and held her arms up towards them in a gesture. The warriors stepped forward and placed the severed heads on the slab or altar.

The whole tribe went silent and watched as Merva seemed to go into a trance, mumbling strange words and holding her hands up towards the moon. Then the warriors who had placed the heads approached one at a time, Merva pored liquid from one of the jugs into a bowl and offered each warrior a drink. After drinking the liquid each warrior picked up a head off the alter and stood facing Merva. She reached into the large bowl that Etain had brought, then touched each warrior on the forehead. Tim could see that what she was putting on their foreheads was blood, before offering a prayer for each one, then they retreated carrying the heads with them. After all the warriors had taken their respective heads and left the circle, Merva took the remainder of the blood in the large bowl and poured it on the ground in a circle around the altar, then said a prayer and gestured to the white robed girls to offer everyone a drink poured from the jugs into the bowls they had brought earlier. The whole tribe processed in order past the altar, took a drink of the brew and filed out of the circle and through the trees. When it was Vortan's turn to take a drink, he approached the altar and took a bowl from one of the white robed girls. Tim was horrified, wondering what was in the bowl. It was just some kind of alcoholic brew. As they left the clearing the girls were singing again as they collected the jugs and bowls and followed the last of the warriors down the path in the woods, across the wooden bridge and just a few yards to the settlement, were they danced and talked into the night around the fires.

Tim shook himself as if from a deep sleep and gasped as he reflected on what he had just witnessed. He couldn't decide whether he was horrified or just amazed at the experience he had just lived through. He turned to Vortan and enquired, "what was all that about?"

"Well," said Vortan, "you did say you wanted to know more about my life, so what do you think?" Tim paused to collect his thoughts. "It was very interesting, but rather gruesome, could you explain to me what was going on?" "Yes," said Vortan, "one of our children came running to the village saying there was a group of Cunai warriors stealing our cattle from their grazing field." "My father prepared a war party and intercepted them, killed the Cunai warriors and brought the cattle back to our village, then we had a ceremony to honour our gods and thank them for the success of our mission." Tim thought for a moment then asked, "Why did they have to die and why did they have their heads cut off and then put on that alter while people danced around chanting?" Vortan replied. "First of all, as far as the Cunai was concerned, if we didn't kill them, they would kill us, and they were stealing our cattle which were more valuable than you could possibly imagine." "It was also normal practice to cut off the enemies heads, for two reasons, firstly, nobody comes back to life when their head is cut off, and secondly, if you cut off their head you can then steal their spirit and add to your strength."

"The ceremony in our sacred grove was to thank the gods for our success also to take away the spirits from the heads of the enemy warriors and transfer them to the warriors that killed them." Tim thought it was all very bloodthirsty and gory. "That place where the ceremony was held, felt very strange!" said Tim, "why was that." Vortan laughed, then replied, "That place as you put it, was our sacred grove called a 'Nemeton' where we held all our religious ceremonies, perhaps it felt strange to you because you've been there before." "What do you mean?" said Tim, puzzled. Vortan laughed again, "That's where you first met me, when you found my axe!" Tim felt a cold shiver run down his back as he pondered the thought of all the time, he'd spent in that place with his metal detector. He reflected on how he even liked it there, how he felt so comfortable in that strange and gruesome place. Perhaps it was because that small part of him had been there before and it was drawing him back, anyway he decided that he would have a very different view of the place in future.

CHAPTER THIRTEEN

THE GROVE AND THE CELTIC GODS

Tim spoke to Vortan again. "The sacred grove, as you put it, doesn't look very sacred now does it?" "No" replied Vortan, "it's overgrown and spoiled now, but we could go and clear it up and put it back as it used to be." Tim thought for a moment. "I don't want to have anything to do with those gruesome ceremonies," he said nervously. Vortan laughed again. "That wasn't what I wanted to clear the place up for," said Vortan. "I just thought that if we cleared it up and put it back as it was, we could keep it as our special place, our sanctuary from the troubles of everyday life, a place where we could just go and relax and forget about all our problems, and perhaps say a little prayer to the gods, so that they may watch over us and keep us from harm." Tim was deep in thought again. "What Gods?" he enquired, "I'm a Catholic and I have been brought up to follow the ways of Christianity, which is to worship Christ and just the one god, I don't know anything about any other gods," he said in a very confused way. "Well," said Vortan, "in my time we had many gods and goddesses, they had their own domains, their own reasons for being." "We also had our own tribal gods that were special to our tribe." "Tell me more about these gods said Tim." "Well," said Vortan, "It's very complicated, there are such a lot of them, but I'll try." "Firstly, there was our own tribal goddess, 'Sull', she was our special protector, she looked after all the members of our tribe, we called on her when we needed healing, not just for the people but also for the animals and the trees and plants." "Then there was 'Nemeton', she was the protector of the sacred grove, the Nemeton, this was our place of worship like a church, but it wasn't a building, it was a grove in the woods with an altar where we made offerings to all the gods, it was the place where you first met me when you found my axe, your favourite place." "Dis, was the father of all our gods." "Lugh, was our god of light and our warrior god." "Sirona, was our goddess of fertility, rebirth and healing." "And Brighde, was our mother goddess, the goddess of fire, the sun, the moon, the animals, the smiths, the family, medicine, music, poetry and war." Tim shook his head in amazement. "That's a lot of gods and goddesses," he said, "how did you keep track of them all." Vortan laughed and replied, "you soon remember which is which when you're in trouble and you need their help, and anyway we were brought up learning all about them, just as you are taught about your Christian god." Tim smiled; he was beginning to understand now. "OK," he said, "we'll go and clear the grove up and make it nice again, if that will make you happy, just as soon as we have some time." "Good." Said Vortan, "That will please the gods, I'm sure they will thank us for remembering them after all this time." Tim thought deep about that idea, he didn't know what to make of it all.

Tim fell into a deep sleep as if he had been into battle himself. He awoke in the morning feeling very much refreshed, but with his head full of most unusual thoughts, as if he been watching a strange film and was very much involved in the film himself. It all seemed quite surreal, and Tim was struggling to take it all in. He decided he would have to put it at the back of his mind for now and get on with living in the present.

CHAPTER FOURTEEN

BACK TO SCHOOL

He quickly washed and dressed and went downstairs to find his mother and granddad sat talking at breakfast. "Good morning you two," said Tim, "and how are you feeling now mother?" Tina smiled through the bruises, "I'm feeling much better today, I think I'll be back to normal in a few days, but granddad has some good news for you, tell him pop," she said as she turned to her father, (Edgar). "Well." said Edgar, "I've been to your school and spoken to your headmaster, and he very kindly said you can return to school just as soon as you're ready and there will be no further action taken against you from the school, so what do you think about that Tim?" Tim thought for a moment. "I'm so excited, I can't wait to get back!" said Tim sarcastically. "I bet," said Tina laughing, "but you need to go back and if they're not going to hold it against you, it should be OK, don't you think Tim?" "I'll believe that when I see it." He spoke. "Anyway, I suppose I'll have to go back some time, so I might as well get on with it,

I'll go and get ready and give it a try today." Edgar was surprised to find Tim so ready to oblige. "Would you like me to come with you Tim.," said Edgar. "No, I'll be fine." Said Tim, "anyway I've already got someone with me, I just hope nobody gets violent again, I've seen enough of that to last me for a lifetime." Tim got ready and set off for school, wondering what kind of reception he would receive.

He certainly wasn't ready for what happened as he stepped onto the bus to get downtown. No sooner had he stepped on to the bus, when almost everyone on the bus started cheering and applauding him. Tim was completely surprised and totally embarrassed, he could feel himself go red and flushed. He looked around the bus until he saw his friend Sam, or as he was better known Hotpot, it was something to do with his favourite food. He went and sat next to him, but people were still making a fuss, patting him on the back as he passed down the bus. "What's going on?" He said to his friend. Hotpot was beaming as he put his arm around Tim. "You're a hero," he said, everyone thinks you're wonderful since you sorted out the Bull-Iggy gang. Tim laughed as he put his arm around Hotpot's shoulders. "It wasn't just me, you helped as well." "I didn't do anything." Said Hotpot, "I just stood and watched." Tim looked at him and said, "The important thing is that you stood your ground, you didn't run off, you must have been scared stiff but you still stood by me, that's what matters, I know you can't fight, but you stayed with me, that takes courage and you're the hero." Hotpot was clearly pleased to hear these words as he snuggled into the corner by the window of the bus. When the bus stopped, and most people trouped off they were once again congratulating Tim and patting him on the back. He found all this adoration very disconcerting, still it was better than being called 'Timid Tim and being laughed at constantly. As Tim and Hotpot stepped off the bus and set off on the short distance to their school they were surrounded by several girls, all wanting to know how Timothy had managed to get to be such a brilliant fighter all of a sudden. Tim thought he would play a game with them and said, he could always fight like that but didn't think it was very clever to hurt people, so he pretended to be a wimp. This just impressed them even more. Now everybody wanted to be Tim and Hotpot's friend.

When they arrived at school and eventually got into class they were greeted with more cheering and clapping, until their teacher (Mr Conway) walked into the room. "Quiet," he shouted, slamming a pile of books down on his desk and scowling at the whole class. Order was eventually achieved and Mr Conway's eye's searched around the class for the cause of the disruption when his stare fixed on Timothy. "Ah, Rocky has come back." This brought a roar of laughter from the whole class. When the noise calmed down Mr Conway spoke to Tim again. "The headmaster would like a word with you Henderson, if it's not too much trouble," 'Go now.' Timothy set of down the corridor thinking here we go again, more trouble. He arrived at the head's office and knocked, "come in," Tim opened the door and walked in expecting more rebuke off the headmaster. He was surprised when Mr Whitfield spoke very polite and courteously to him and welcomed him back, saying, if there were any further problems he would be pleased if Tim would bring them to him and hoped that he could settle down to some useful studying. Tim was amazed and agreed promptly. As he left the head's office, he couldn't help wondering what his granddad had said to him to create such a change, anyway things were looking better than when he was here last.

As Timothy stepped out of the headmaster's office, he paused to reflect on how his life had changed in the last two weeks, in fact since he met his other self, Vortan, he was beginning to feel rather pleased with himself. Before he met Vortan he had a thoroughly miserable existence, bullied at school, laughed at by the other pupils, bullied at home by his drunk of a stepfather, having to stand by and watch his beautiful mother being beaten senseless by him. Now the bullies at school were, well, not in a position to bully anyone, the other kids were not laughing at him anymore and his thug of a stepfather was now dead, and his mother was on the mend. Timothy felt happy for the first time in years. At playtime Tim and his mate, Hotpot went into the yard, hotpot was desperate to talk to Tim about the strange transformation that has taken place. Unfortunately, he didn't get chance because they become surrounded by other pupils, mostly girls, all wanting to talk to the two friends. All wanting to be their friends. Tim and Hotpot were most surprised by all this attention, they had both been virtually invisible before and nobody was interested in anything they had to say or what they were doing. Now everyone wanted to know all about the two friends, and what they had to say, what they did in their spare time, in fact everything about them. It was very strange but quite pleasant for the two friends. Eventually they managed get away from all the attention and get some space for themselves. Hotpot was very keen to find out what had actually happened to Tim, to turn him into such a fearless fighter all of a sudden. "Come on tell me, what's happened to you," he said to Timothy. Tim laughed and said, "It's no use, you won't believe me if I tell you, it's too ridiculous." "Try me," said Hotpot, "I'm pretty gullible." Tim thought for a moment, "come to my house tonight and I'll try and explain, but I'm sure you won't believe me."

After school Tim went straight home, he was anxious to see how his mother was fairing after her ordeal, his grandfather had to go home at lunchtime and Tim was concerned about her being on her own. He was so pleased to see that she looked as if there had been no injuries at all, she smiled as Tim walked in. "You look fantastic," said Tim, "How do you feel," "I feel really good," said Tina, "I feel as if the gods are looking after me and helping me to recover." "The gods?" said Tim, questioningly. "Vortan's gods," said Tina, "I can really feel a presence here since Vortan came to join us." Tim couldn't deny that his mother looked wonderful considering the injuries she had sustained just a couple of weeks since, but he still felt dubious about the idea of ancient Celtic gods being involved.

After tea Tim went into the garden shed to find some tools for clearing up Vortan's grove, a two-handed sickle, a small spade and a pair of pruning shears. He was about to set off for the woods when Hotpot turned up, but he wasn't alone, he had with him, one of the girls from their class at St Josephs, her name was Rebecca and she lived not far from Tim. He looked at her then turned to Hotpot, "what's going on?" said Tim. "Rebecca wants to come and hang out for a while, she says she knows what we have been through, as she has been bullied for years at school and she was delighted when you put a stop to the Bull-Iggy gang." Tim looked at Rebecca, she was quite a pretty girl, but a bit overweight and wore glasses, she was taller than both

Tim and Hotpot and she had the most beautiful wavy jet-black hair down to her waist. She had been teased about her weight a lot and didn't enjoy school very much at all. Tim was very confused; they had never had a girl for a friend before. "We're going to the woods to do some work, clearing up, are you sure you want to come, it might get a bit grubby you know." Rebecca laughed, "I can do more work than you two put together." She spoke. "OK," said Tim, "let's go." "Clearing up," said Hotpot, "when did I agree to that, you said you would explain about what's happened to you to bring about such a change." "Later," said Tim, "when we get to the wood, I'll try, but I don't think you'll believe me anyway." He said.

CHAPTER FIFTEEN

FRIENDS MEETING VORTAN

The three friends set out for Vortan's wood, Tim had already been to see the farmer Mr Bickerstaff and his wife, the day before to ask if he could do a bit of clearing in the wood so he could play there. They said that would be fine so long as he didn't cut any trees down. Mr Bickerstaff and his wife were very fond of Tim, they were always pleased to see him, they had no children of their own. They had a son, but he died when he was three and although he would have been much older than Tim by now, they liked to make a fuss of Tim. He often had dinner with them on Sundays and they always gave him presents for birthdays and Christmas. Tim had been given permission to use his metal detector all over the farm so long as he didn't damage any crops. The wood was part of the farm and Tim spent a lot of his time in there. When the three friends arrived at the wood, Hotpot couldn't wait to start climbing trees, he wasn't very big, but he was a brilliant climber, he just loved shinning up trees and shouting from up in the branches,

Rebecca wasn't so keen on climbing though. Tim called to Hotpot, hey we're supposed to be doing some work, not climbing trees, get down here now. Hotpot was down in a few seconds, he was only small, but he was as fit as a flea and could tumble about like a gymnast, he really was funny to watch and he had been such a good friend to Tim since they had both been in infants school together. They all came together, and Tim explained what needed to be done, so they set about clearing the weeds and small bushes. They worked for about an hour and a half, but it was getting dark, so they had a sit down on a large slab of sandstone before setting off for home. Hotpot turned to Tim, "we're still waiting for an explanation Tim," he said. Tim was obviously stalling. "OK," he said, "hear goes." "A few weeks ago, when I was searching here with my metal detector, I found this bronze axe head, he reached into his shoulder bag and produced Vortan's axe. This is two thousand seven hundred years old, and it belonged to a Celtic warrior called Vortan." Hotpot and Rebecca both looked very confused. "How do you know it belonged to a warrior called Vortan?" Asked Rebecca. "Because he appeared in front of me, right there, by that log where I found the axe." "You're having us on, aren't you," said Hotpot. "I knew you wouldn't believe me," said Tim. "Well, it is a bit farfetched, isn't it?" said Hotpot. Rebecca was laughing out loud. Tim turned his thoughts to Vortan and silently asked, "What do you think, can we show them?" "OK," said Vortan, "but you will need to prepare them for the shock." Tim asked his friends, "would you like to meet Vortan?" "Yes of course," they both said mockingly. Tim stood up in front his two friends and gestured for them to turn round. As they turned, they both leapt back and fell onto the soft leafy ground, as they lay there with their mouths wide open. "Oh my god," said Rebecca, in total shock. "No," said Tim, "that's not god, it's Vortan," "I did warn you, didn't I?" Vortan was stood there in all his war paint, spear in one hand, bronze sword in the other, he looked very fierce and frightening. "Well," said Tim, "What do you think now, do you believe?" His two friends were speechless, but they managed to nod their heads, mainly in fright. Tim spoke to Vortan, "Do you think you could get rid of the war paint now and let them see you without? In a blink Vortan was stood there without his war paint, bronzed, shining, muscles gleaming, blonde hair down past his shoulders, he stepped forward and held out his hands to Rebecca and Hotpot to help them up off the ground. They were very hesitant until Vortan smiled at them and insisted they take his hand. As they stood up, they were shaking with shock. Tim reassured them that they were not in any danger, as Vortan disappeared. "Where has he gone?" asked Rebecca, in a startled voice. "Where do you think he's gone?" said Tim laughing. "I haven't got a clue," said Rebecca, shaking her head. "And what are you laughing at Tim?" "Well." Said Tim "I'll give you a clue, how do you think I managed to sort out the Bull-Iggy gang?" "What does that mean?" asked Hotpot. "It means," said Tim, "that Vortan is in me, That I am now Vortan, he has been reincarnated into me, and as Vortan was the greatest warrior of his time, I have inherited his ability to fight, so putting it simply, we are not taking any more bullying off anyone ever again."

Hotpot and Rebecca looked at Tim in disbelief, but after what they had just seen, they had little choice but to accept Tim's story. It was now getting quite dark, and the three friends made their way home. It had been quite a day.

On the way home Timothy tried to explain to Hotpot and Rebecca as much as he could about Vortan and his life, he didn't feel very comfortable talking about what happened to Duncan, so he steered clear of the subject. Timothy was pleased that he had come together with Vortan, but he was rather concerned that there was a dark side to Vortan that he had absolutely no control over.

Back at home Tim's mother, Tina told him the police had been and told her that they were releasing Duncan's body so they could arrange his funeral. Tim had no kind feelings for Duncan after all the violence, both he and his mother had suffered at his hands, he was a drunken bully and Tim was glad to see the back of him, but he was happy to help his mother sort out the funeral arrangements.

Next day at school Tim met Hotpot and Rebecca and impressed upon them not to talk about Vortan and what they had seen the night before. "Don't worry," said Rebecca, "if we told people what had happened to us last night, they'd probably laugh their heads off, or send for the school nurse." "Good," said Tim, "let's keep it to ourselves then." "Are we going to do some more work in the wood tonight," said Hotpot. "OK," said Tim, "if you want to, what about you Rebecca, are you coming or did last night frighten you too much?" "Try and stop me," said Rebecca, "I've never been so excited about anything in my life." "Right," said Tim, "come to my house at five O clock and we'll get going." The three friends were happy to have formed a bond and made a pact together, also with a new interest in clearing their woodland grove.

RESTORING THE GROVE

That evening they all got busy working away in the wood. The whole place was beginning to take shape with all the weeds and small bushes cleared, any loose stones put in one pile at the side, and the grass roughly cut with the sickle. "How are we going to move this large flat stone?" said Rebecca, "it's much too heavy for us to move, it must weigh at least a Ton." Tim looked at Rebecca and smiled. "That's not going anywhere," he said. "But it's right in the middle of the clearing," insisted Rebecca. "That's where it's supposed to be," declared Tim, remembering the layout of the Nemeton from his dreamlike vision." "Really," said Rebecca, "why, what is it supposed to be?" Tim called Hotpot and Rebecca together to explain the history and use of the clearing. "It's called a Nemeton," said Tim, "which means a sacred grove, to the ancient Celts, and that large flat stone is the altar where they used to make offerings to their gods.

Rebecca and Hotpot stared at the stone and felt a chill run down their backs as they quizzed Tim about what kind of offerings. "I'll explain about that later," said Tim, "but for now let's just clear around it and underneath to see what sort of condition it's in." The stone slab seemed to be resting on a small mound of earth about three feet high, but when they started clearing around it with the spade, they realised it wasn't resting on a mound of earth, it was actually resting on two pedestal type stones. It took quite some time to clear all the earth from around and underneath the structure but when the job was done it became clear that it was an altar, and it gave a quite different atmosphere to the clearing. The three friends stepped back and looked at their handy work, they had worked extremely hard and were quite pleased with the result, and the special place was beginning to look very different. "What next," asked Hotpot, as he stretched himself up and pulled his shoulders back in satisfaction?" "Well," said Tim, "we need some logs to place on the floor to sit on, I'll ask the farmer, Mr Bickerstaff if we can have some, there are some behind the barn." "Do you really think he'll let us have some," said Rebecca, "it's a bit cheeky isn't it?" Tim laughed, "Not really Mr Bickerstaff is a very kind man, and he has given me permission to clear this area and use it for my special place, I'll ask him to bring us some logs with his tractor, I'm sure it will be alright." It was going dark and Tim, Hotpot and Rebecca, set off for home, tired but very pleased with their achievements. "I wonder what Vortan thinks about the place now?" Said Rebecca. "He is very happy about it," said Tim.

On the way home Tim told his friends he needed to take a day off school tomorrow in order to help his mother arrange Duncan's funeral. He said he would also call and see Mr Bickerstaff and ask him about some logs for the grove. He suggested that they should all go back to the grove tomorrow evening, not to work but to just relax and enjoy the place and he would explain more about Vortan and his life. He told his friends he was very grateful for their help and support and all their hard work.

Next day Tim went with his mother downtown, it was the first time she had been out since leaving hospital. Tim was concerned whether she was recovered enough to be out, but Tina assured him she felt fine. After making arrangements for Duncan's funeral and doing some shopping Timothy and his mother Tina returned home by lunch time. Tim insisted she rest on the couch and have a sleep as she was obviously quite tired, even though she wouldn't admit it.

After getting his mother settled, Tim jumped on his bike and set off on the short distance to Tarbock to see his friends the Bickerstaff's' and ask if he could have three or four logs for his grove. Mrs Bickerstaff was a large slim woman with silver hair, she had been blonde when she was younger, she was a cheerful woman always smiling and very pleasant. "Hello Tim, come on in, how are you doing, and why aren't you at school today?" She said in a happy voice. "I've been downtown with my mother to arrange Duncan's funeral." Said Tim. "Ah, I see, and how is you mother after coming out of hospital?" asked the farmer's wife. "She's doing very well under the circumstances, I've left her having a sleep on the couch," said Tim. "You've both had a difficult time with that Duncan, haven't you, I bet you're glad to see the back of him?" Tim just nodded. Mrs Bickerstaff gave Tim a hug and kissed him on the cheek. "Never mind Tim, it's all over now, you don't have to put up with him anymore, I'm sure your life will get better from now on," she said. "I've just made some fresh cakes, so you can have one and a cup of tea, and I'll give Jack a call, he'll be delighted to see you. Tim was enjoying his cup of tea and cake when Mr Bickerstaff came in. "Hi Tim, how's your project in the wood coming along?" he said with a smile. Tim nodded with his mouth full of cake, then took a swig of tea. "Do you think I could have three or four of those logs for my place in the wood, just for sitting on?" "Of course you can," said the farmer, "if you come with me now and give me a hand, we'll put the forks on the tractor and take them over for you." "Thank you," said Tim smiling.

After fitting the forks to the tractor Tim selected four logs from the pile at the rear of the barn, they were off trees the farmer had cut down two years ago while clearing the top field for planting. "Just two at a time," said Mr Bickerstaff, "they're very heavy you know, anymore and they would tip the tractor up." They took the first two logs along the track to the edge of the woods and across the stone bridge, not the one in Tim's vision of the place in ancient times, this bridge was a modern one, then into Tim's clearing. "My goodness," said Mr Bickerstaff, "you have been busy, haven't you? You've done an excellent job hear, how on earth did you manage all this? Tim laughed, "I had some help from my two friends, Hotpot and Rebecca, they've worked very hard with me to tidy the place up, I hope you don't mind." The farmer burst out laughing. "Hotpot, he said, "what sort of a name is that?" Tim laughed, "His name is Sam, but everyone calls him hotpot, he's my best friend." The farmer was still laughing, "I don't mind at all Tim, both me and the Missus are always pleased to see you and you're not doing any harm," he said cheerfully, "but you do know this place is very strange, don't you?" "What do you mean," said Tim quizzically?" "Well, some people say that this place is haunted you know, and some say it's actually cursed," said the farmer. "I think it's a beautiful place," said Tim. "So do I," said Mr Bickerstaff, "and as long as you're happy here, that's fine by me. They placed all four logs in position and Tim thanked the farmer for his help and for allowing him to use the place, then Tim picked up his bike and set off for home. Tim was pleased to see his mother happily pottering about the house in a cheerful mood. She smiled at Tim as she spoke, "Where have you been?" she asked. "I've been to the farm to do a little work," he said, "Mr and Mrs Bickerstaff asked about you, and send their regards." "Oh, that's nice of them, especially since I've never met them," said Tim's mother. "Well, they would like to meet you some time, they're very nice people you know, and they have given me permission to tidy up Vortan's grove, Mr Bickerstaff has even helped me and given me some logs, it's looking quite nice now," said Tim. "Oh really," said Tina, and what do they know about Vortan?" "Nothing," said Tim, "I just asked if I could clear the place up, to play in."

Next day at school Tim and Hotpot went to find Rebecca in the playground. They were annoyed to see that she was being tormented by a gang of girls from her class. "What's going on?" said Tim to the gang of bullies, in an aggressive voice. "We're just having a bit of fun, Tim," said one of the girls. "Oh really," said Tim, "well go and have fun somewhere else and leave Rebecca alone." The gang of girls skulked off to the other side of the playground. Since Tim's violent encounter with the Bull-Iggy gang, nobody in the school wanted to cross Tim or his friends. "Thanks," said Rebecca, "They're always having a go at me." "Not anymore," said Tim, "We're not taking any more bullying from anyone." "Anyway, let's talk about Vortan's grove, I've been and put some logs around and it's looking good now, so are we going over there tonight?" Rebecca and Hotpot both agreed so the three friends arranged to meet at Tim's after tea. Tim said they didn't need any tools today, so they all set off for the woods.

CHAPTER SEVENTEEN

THE GROVE COMES TO LIFE

As they approached their grove they received the most incredible surprise, even though it was September the whole of the grove was alight with the most beautiful vision of colour, bluebells covered the whole of the clearing floor, all around the edges of the clearing there were beautiful varieties of blossoms on trees, white, pink and purple, the whole place looked like a picture from a calendar. Even the birds had taken a liking to the place, there were sky larks singing, swallows diving about to have a look at the place, sparrows singing in the trees, there was even a family of rabbits playing at the far end of the grove. The three friends stood speechless, amazed at the sight before them. "How did you do all this?" said Rebecca turning to Tim. Tim burst out laughing. "It wasn't me, all I did yesterday was bring the logs with Mr Bickerstaff's help, it wasn't like this when I left last night, I don't understand." "Well then, what's happened to make the place like this?"

said Hotpot. Tim went noticeably quiet and distant for a while as Vortan spoke to him within.

"The gods have smiled on you, this is their way of showing you that they are very pleased with what you have done to their sacred grove, you my friend, have been highly honoured by the gods of the grove." "They have been very much ignored for such a long time now, and you and your friends have paid them a tribute by restoring the grove, you are all very much in their favour, you should be very happy." Said Vortan. Tim explained to Hotpot and Rebecca what Vortan had just told him. They were happy but somewhat confused. They couldn't get their heads around the idea of lots of gods, but they did know that there was some very special power in play here, they had never seen anything like it before, so they agreed to reserve judgement on where the power came from. In the meantime, they all ran round the grove, jumping and shouting, incredibly pleased with their efforts and just loving the place. Hotpot climbing trees as usual, Rebecca just dancing around singing with the birds, and Tim laughing at the top of his voice. When they had all calmed down and got over the initial shock, Tim said, "I must go and bring Mr and Mrs Bickerstaff and show them what's happened, they're never going to believe this unless they see it for themselves.

Tim ran the short distance to the farmhouse and knocked on the door. "Come in.," shouted Mrs Bickerstaff. "Hello Tim," she said as Tim opened the door, "what's the matter you look all exited?" "Please come and look what's happened to the grove, it's beautiful, tell Mr Bickerstaff, said Tim, he couldn't contain his excitement. The farmer's wife called her husband, and they all hurried to the grove. As they crossed the bridge and hurried along the short track to the entrance to the grove both the farmer and his wife stopped in their tracks as they gazed in wonder at the sight before them. "Good grief," said the farmer, that's amazing, while his wife put her arm around Tim's shoulder and kissed him on the forehead, and spoke, with tears running down her cheeks, "this is all your doing Tim, You've brought sunshine to this dark wood, just like you've brought sunshine to all our lives after years of sadness. Tim was embarrassed but incredibly pleased with himself. Mr Bickerstaff looked at Rebecca and Hotpot and smiled, I suppose this is your gang, is it?" he said to Tim. "Yes," said Tim, this is Rebecca, and this is Hotpot." Both Mr Bickerstaff and his wife burst out laughing, "What sort of a name is Hotpot?" the farmer said laughing. Hotpot replied, well when I was little I was ill and couldn't or wouldn't eat anything, and my parents were worried about me dying, then my grandmother made me some hotpot and it was the only thing I would eat for months, so I suppose it saved my life, so that's why I got the name." Mrs Bickerstaff gave Hotpot a hug and said, "that's a lovely story and it's a lovely name, and we're very pleased to meet you, and you Rebecca, you must all come and have dinner on Sunday, and Tim you should invite your mother, we would love to meet her." Tim thought for a moment then replied, "Why don't we have a picnic in the grove?" he said. "That's a good idea," said Mrs Bickerstaff, "but it is September and a little chilly for picnics, but I'll tell you what, if it's a nice day, we'll have a picnic anyway." "Yes," they all shouted.

They all went home very happy; it had been an extremely interesting day. When Tim arrived home, he told his mother what had happened. She was pleased, especially that Tim had found some friends and that he had become much stronger and more assertive, he was also a very much happier boy since he had joined with Vortan. Both their lives were starting to take on a completely different meaning. Tim also told his mother about their Sunday picnic and that the Bickerstaff's' had invited her, he explained that they were looking forward to meeting her. She said she would be happy to go and meet them but them explained to Tim that Duncan's funeral was to be on Friday and that she wanted him to attend. Tim was very hesitant about this but agreed in order to please and support his mother. Also, he thought it would give them the opportunity to put the memory of Duncan behind them and look to the future without him.

CHAPTER EIGHTEEN

THE PICNIC

Having got Duncan's funeral out of the way and Tina now recovered quite wonderfully. Sunday arrived and Tim was very excited about the picnic and the idea of getting together with all his favourite people. The weather was particularly fine for September and the grove was even more lively and colourful than when they were last there. When Tim and his mother arrived at the grove, she stood transfixed in amazement, looking at the beautiful array of blooms and blossoms and listening to the birds singing, "It's like paradise," she said. "How did you do all this?" "We didn't," said Tim, "we just tidied the place up, the gods did the rest according to Vortan." "Well, he would know, wouldn't he?" declared Tina. She walked all around the grove as Tim went off to help Mr and Mrs Bickerstaff with the baskets of goodies for the picnic. Rebecca and Hotpot had already arrived but were exploring the woods around the grove, when they saw Tim's mum in the grove, they ran to greet her. Tina had only recently met them both and was incredibly pleased that Tim had made friends and started to mix a little. Rebecca and Hotpot were very keen to show Tina all around the grove and explain about what they had done, and how the place looked before they started, they were immensely proud of their handy work.

Meanwhile Tim was at the farmhouse helping Mrs Bickerstaff load the food into the two large baskets, lots of sandwiches, homemade sausage rolls and meat pies, and Tim's special favourite, a wide variety of home-made cakes. Mr Bickerstaff was filling another basket with fresh fruit; he had also brought from the cellar a large stone jar of cider. "I hope you've got some soft drinks for the children said Mrs Bickerstaff, looking at the cider jar." "Of course," said Mr Bickerstaff, "are we all ready now, we don't want to keep the others waiting, do we?" Tim asked if they could take a small table to put the food on. "Of course," said Mrs Bickerstaff, "but there's that stone table there already, can't we use that to put the food on, she said?" "That's not a table," said Tim, without thinking. The farmer and his wife both looked at Tim in surprise. "What is it then?" they enquired. Tim hesitated, he realised he'd said the wrong thing, "What is it Tim, if it's not a table?" they insisted. "It's an altar, I think," declared Tim nervously. "What do you mean, an altar" asked Mrs Bickerstaff. "Well," said Tim realising he'd put his foot in it, "I think that place is an ancient grove called a Nemeton which is like a modern day church, and the stone slab in the centre is the altar, so I don't think we should use it for our table, in respect for those people of the past." Mrs Bickerstaff smiled and stroked Tim's hair back. "You are a funny boy; OK we'll take a table." They loaded the baskets and a folding table on to a small trailer attached to the small tractor.

Tim and Mrs Bickerstaff sat on the trailer and rode the short distance to the grove. The farmer and his wife were delighted to meet Tim's mother, they told her that Tim had brought such sunshine into their life, as they had been rather sad since the death of their own son some years earlier. Tina was pleased to meet Mr and Mrs Bickerstaff and told them that Timothy had become much happier since he had started coming here. They were all rather hungry by now and got busy putting the table up and spreading the food out on it. It was a fine September day, and they were all enjoying the occasion, chatting and joking, and commenting on how beautiful the grove looked since Tim and his friends had cleared it up. While everyone was busy chatting and eating, Tim went to the table and selected some fruit, put it on a paper plate and took it over to the stone altar and placed it in the centre. When he turned round, he realised everyone was watching him. "What is that for?" asked his mother. "Well," said Tim," we are all having such a good time, and the grove is so beautiful now, I think it's fitting that we make an offering to the gods that made it all possible." They all looked at one another and raised their eyebrows, but they thought they would humour him anyway. Apart from timothy's weird behaviour, everyone had a wonderful time and after finishing off the stone jar of cider, Mr and Mrs Bickerstaff and Tina were quite merry. They were all happy as they made their way home. All in all, the whole day had been a very enjoy. e experience for everyone concerned, and Tim was particularly pleased with himself. He hoped the gods were also pleased.

Tim retired to bed and turned his thoughts to Vortan. He asked him what he thought about the day, and the idea of his friends having a picnic there. "The gods are very happy with you, you shouldn't need ask." "Why not?" asked Tim. "Well," said Vortan, "if the gods had not been pleased, you and your friends wouldn't have stayed in the grove for very long, the gods would have driven you all out very quickly." "Really," said Tim. "There is something else," said Vortan. "I don't think you realise how much the gods have smiled upon you." "I don't understand," said Tim, "What do you mean?" "The Nemeton, or Grove," said Vortan in it's original state and use, was not covered in flowers and blossoms, and there were no birds singing in there, and there were no animals, playing in there, Rabbits or otherwise, they stayed well away from the Nemeton." "Why was that?" asked Tim. "Because" said Vortan, "The Nemeton was a dark and serious place, where offerings were made to the gods, and animals stayed well clear of the place, and there were no flowers or blossoms growing there, in fact nothing grew there." Tim thought for a moment. "When you say they made offerings in the Nemeton, what exactly do you mean?" said Tim. "We don't want to go into all that stuff just now, said Vortan." Tim felt a cold chill spread over him. "Do you mean what I think you mean?" he said. "That depends on what you think I mean," said Vortan. Tim thought seriously for a moment, then replied. "I am getting the feeling that you mean sacrifices!" "I do not mean sacrifices, I mean offerings; but some of the ceremonies were a bit bloody and gruesome, but we did not sacrifice either people or animals."

"When we killed our enemies, we cut off their heads and took their spirits in a ceremony and offered our thanks to our gods, they were not sacrifices." "Nevertheless, they were bloody and gruesome events, and the grove was always an eerie place and children certainly didn't play there then, nor animals, nor birds, the ground and especially the stone altar were soaked in the blood of our enemies."

"perhaps now you will understand what I mean when I say that the gods have smiled upon you," "You and your friends have changed the place from a dark and eerie place, into a beautiful bright and cheerful place of fun, you have also reawakened the old gods who have been neglected and forgotten about for thousands of years." "This perhaps, is why they have smiled on you and your efforts, by making the flowers and blossoms grow, and also changed the aura of the place to invite the animals and birds into the grove." "Whether you like or not Tim, you are now the master of the grove, and more importantly, the friend of the gods." "It also appears that I have been chosen to help you." Timothy found this news exceedingly difficult to take in. "Best sleep on it," he thought.

Next morning Tim awoke early feeling pleased with himself, he had had a wonderful day with all his favourite people, except for his granddad, 'Edgar' I wish he could have been with us he thought. He lives a few miles away, but never mind, perhaps next time. Tim went down to breakfast and was greeted by his mother. She looked happy and in great spirits, she seemed like her old self, cheerful and smiling. "Good morning, Tim," said Tina, "how do you feel today?" "I feel really good after a sleep I was very tired last night," said Tim. "It was a wonderful day, and everyone had a lovely time, all because of you and your efforts, you should be proud of yourself," said Tina, "because I am." "You have been blessed, and you have brought real happiness to everyone around you, since you found Vortan," she said. "Not everyone," said Tim, "there are a few thugs at school, who have been in hospital, who would like to see me disappear." "Let's hope they've learned their lesson, and leave you alone," said Tina. Timothy nodded as he kissed his mother and set off for school.

CHAPTER NINETEEN

REBECCA'S GOOD NEWS

Monday morning and Tim and Hotpot were surprised that Rebecca didn't turn up at school, so after school they called at her house to see if she was alright. Rebecca was pleased to see Tim and Hotpot, but she looked different. "Why weren't you at school today? And what's happened to your glasses?" asked Tim. "I haven't been wearing them all day," said Rebecca. "I don't know what's happened, but I don't seem to need them just now, my eyesight has improved so much, and I can see perfectly well without them," she said. "That's strange," said Tim. Rebecca put her hand on Tim's shoulder and said warmly, "I've never enjoyed myself so much as I did yesterday, it was like a dream, having a picnic in a magic garden, and everybody having such a happy time." "Good," said Tim, "we'll do it again soon." It wasn't just her eyesight that had changed, Rebecca looked much more confident and self-assured. She seemed to stand up taller and smile more. The next day the bus arrived, and they both stepped on.

Rebecca was surprised that the girls were being particularly nice to her and remarking on how she looked without her specs. Tim found Hotpot and sat next to him. "How are you doing mate?" he asked. "I'm fine," replied Hotpot, "but have you seen who's on the bus?" "No," said Tim. "Two of Bull-Iggy's gang, they must be starting back today." Then the bus stopped and who should get on. Bull-Iggy himself. "Don't worry," Tim said to Hotpot, "They won't be in any condition to give us trouble." Then, just as the Bull was approaching their seat, Tim jumped up and stood in front of him. Bull-Iggy stepped back and put his hands up in front of his face. "I don't want any trouble," he said. "Trouble," said Tim sarcastically, "I was just offering you my seat, old friend." "No thanks," said the Bull sheepishly, "they've saved me one at the back." Tim smiled and sat back down. "What are you doing?" growled Hotpot, "are you trying to make him kick off again?" "It's alright," said Tim, "I'm just showing him we're not taking any more nonsense of them anymore," There was a lot of mumbling on the bus from the other pupils, they also thought Tim was going to hit the Bull again. In school everything was going very well and there was no further trouble from the Bull-Iggy gang, at least not for the moment. It heavily rained all day, so Tim and Hotpot decided to stay in and catch up on their homework.

Next day Tim met Rebecca at the bus stop, and she couldn't wait to tell him what the optician had said, she was very excited. "He said he didn't know how it had happened but my eyesight was now perfect, and I didn't need to wear glasses any more, he said it was amazing, he couldn't explain it," "so what do you think about that Tim?" she said, "isn't it great?" "That's brilliant," said Tim.

"I think it's something to do with the grove," he said deep in thought. "Really," said Rebecca, "how do you mean?" "Well, it seems the ancient gods are pleased with us for restoring the grove and spending time there and want to show us their favour."

He went on. "In ancient times the grove was a place of worship, but also a place where the tribal people made offerings to the gods." "Times have changed now, and we're not going to offer any blood or cut any heads off our enemies, but they're pleased because we restored the grove, and I did make them an offering of fruit just as a gesture." "In return it seems they have given us their blessing and turned the grove into a place of healing and happiness." "But please don't go round telling people, or it will be ruined for us." Rebecca thought about this for a moment.

It was a bit farfetched, but she couldn't deny that the grove did seem magical, and her eyesight had been really poor all her life, and had become perfect overnight, and there was the strange appearance of Vortan. She decided that, until a better explanation came along, she would go along with Tim's theory. Anyway, she had to admit that since she had been hanging out with Tim and Hotpot, her life, and not just her eyesight had dramatically improved. The other girls had stopped bullying her, and she felt not just happier, but also, fitter and stronger. She walked around with her head held high and her shoulders pulled back, in fact she looked so much better than she had just a short time before. Yes, life is sweet, she thought. "OK," she said to Tim, "I'll buy that for now, but it is a bit mad, isn't it?" she said, staring questioningly at Tim. "Just don't go round telling everyone, "Said Tim. "Are you kidding?" said Rebecca, "they'd put me in a mental home if I went round saying things like that." Tim smiled as they boarded the bus for school. Tim sat with hotpot, and Rebecca sat at the back with a few girls, they chatted happily on the way downtown.

CHAPTER TWENTY

TROUBLE FOR BULL-IGGY

The three friends walked the short distance together from the bus stop to school chatting away happily but as they approached the school gates they noticed two men in their twenties standing there, they seemed to be waiting for someone, Tim paused to look at the two men then looked seriously at Rebecca and Hotpot. "What is it," asked Hotpot. "Trouble," said Tim, thoughtfully. "How do you know?" asked Rebecca. "It's in their faces," said Tim. "Never mind," he said, "let's get in school, it's not our problem," They all agreed and went into school.

At break time the three friends were walking around the school yard discussing what they were going to do at weekend. Tim said," we need to go and do some work in the grove, and also, I want to do some metal detecting around the woods outside the grove. Hotpot and Rebecca were just about to agree when they were approached by Bull-Iggy. Tim turned to meet him square on and stepped forward. "Please," said the Bull, hesitantly, "I don't want any trouble."

"What do you want?" said Tim, firmly. "I'm in trouble, and I need some help, and I was wondering if you would give me a chance to explain?" "Why would we want to help you?" Said Tim. Bull-Iggy shrugged his shoulders and lowered his head. He looked a totally different person to the thug who ruled the school with violence and intimidation just a short time ago. "Well, it was your doing that got me into this situation, when you put me and the others in hospital." "What do you mean by that?" said Tim.

Bull-Higgy was hesitant but eventually replied. "Before I went into hospital, I used to sell gear, and I don't want to do it anymore." Tim looked at him sternly. "You mean you used to sell drugs?" Bull-Iggy nodded shamefully. "Then don't do it," said Tim. "I wish it was that simple," said the Bull." Tim thought for a moment, then replied. "The two men at the school gates this morning?" he said quizzically. "That's right," said Bull-Iggy, "They told me if I don't start dealing again, they'll beat me up and put me back in hospital, and the truth is, since fighting with you I haven't got the nerve anymore, I just don't think I could handle the violence again, I just don't know what to do." Tim looked at Hotpot and Rebecca, they shrugged their shoulders, they didn't know what to make of it all. He turned to Bull-Iggy. "What is it you want from us?" he said. "You mean you'll help me?" He spoke. Tim nodded. "Oh thanks, I'll make it up to you, I promise." "Just understand," said Tim, "If you're not being straight with us, you'll get worse from me than you would from them." "I'm being straight with you, I know what you did to my dad, and I don't want any more trouble with you, I promise, I want to change," said the Bull." "I've just got a few months before I leave school, and I simply want to get on with my exams and put it all behind me, and if you help me I'll never forget you for it and I'll pay you back some way, I promise."

"OK," said Tim, "Tell us what's going down." "They're going to be waiting for me at the gates after school today to give me the gear, and if I don't agree they're going to beat me up," said Bull-Iggy. "We'll see you later," said Tim, "don't worry."

Tim turned his thoughts to Vortan and asked him what he thought about the idea of helping Bull-Iggy. "You should follow your conscience, and do what you think is the right thing," said Vortan. "OK," said Tim, "but will you be there to help," "Of course," said Vortan, "whatever problems you have, we'll face them together, but you should understand that when you go into battle there is no guarantee what the outcome will be, also those two men carry weapons, I don't know what weapons but they do carry them." "How do you know that?" asked Tim. "I spent my whole life fighting," said Vortan, "I just know, so we must be prepared." "How do we do that?" said Tim. "I'll explain and you can get the others organised beforehand, said Vortan.

During the afternoon break Tim called Bull-Iggy, Rebecca and Hotpot together and gave them instructions on the plans for dealing with the drug dealers, he insisted that they must stick to the plan to the letter and that they need to have courage. He wished them all luck.

After school Tim and Hotpot cut across the school field to the wooded pathway that runs alongside the school, called woodland walk. The walk is lined on both sides with trees, Oak, Sycamore, Elm and others, there are lots of bushes there also. They climbed the iron fence and waited behind a large oak tree. Tim gave instructions to Hotpot about exactly how he should behave. Bull-Iggy walked towards the gate where the two men were waiting, Rebecca walked about fifteen yards behind him, appearing not to show any interest in him. The two men were stood on the opposite side of the road scrutinising all the pupils as they passed through the gates. They were both large men, one larger than the other, the taller man was thin with long black hair in a ponytail, he wore a black leather jacket and jeans. The other man was quite tall but heavier with his head shaved and wore a lot of heavy jewellery, necklace, bracelet and hearings, he also had a tattoo on his neck of a bird, just below his left hear. Bull-Iggy looked at them as he passed through the gate to make sure that they had seen him, but then he turned sharp right and took off running down Woodland Walk. The two men at once set off after him. Rebecca stood at the school gate and took out her mobile phone. She dialled emergency and asked for the police and told them that two nasty looking men had chased a boy down Woodland Walk. Meanwhile Bull-iggy continued running down the path with the two drug dealers in hot pursuit. As the Bull passed the spot where Tim and Hotpot were waiting, Hotpot jumped out in front of the two men, waving his arms and jumping up and down, and making the most ridiculous noise. "Get out of the way you little idiot." The ponytailed man shouted, but before he could say anymore, he slumped to the ground and rolled over, Tim was stood over him, then before the baldy man had chance to realise what was happening, he was also struck on the side of the head. He crumbled to the ground and lay motionless. They were both unconscious, Hotpot noticed Tim was holding a large duck stone, Tim wiped the stone on his jumper and threw it into the bushes.

"OK," said Tim to Hotpot, "Let's go before the police get here." The two friends ran down the path to catch up with Bull-Iggy. "what's happened?" said the Bull, "It's OK," said Tim, "they're out of action, just go home and if the police ask you, just tell them that the two men wanted you to sell drugs and you refused and ran off, and that's all you know." The Bull looked at Tim and Hotpot, there were tears in his eyes, as he held out his hand. "I'll never forget what you've done for me, thanks."

Two police officers arrived and ran down Woodland Walk until they found the two men, they were still unconscious, and the officers called for an ambulance and more help. Tim and hotpot cut across the fields to the bus stop where they found Rebecca. "What happened?" said Rebecca, "I saw the police arrive and go down the path, is Bull-Iggy alright?" "He's OK," said Tim. "Just relax and let's not talk about it where we can be overheard." "Let's meet at five O Clock and we can go to the grove, we can talk there. They all caught the bus home. It had been an eventful day.

Later as the three friends walked to the grove talking, Hotpot remarked, "Don't you think that what happened this afternoon was a bit violent?" "Of course it was," said Tim. "What did you expect?" "What did happen?" asked Rebecca. "Shall I, or will you tell her?" said Hotpot. "You tell her, "Said Tim. "Well, when we got the two thugs to chase Bull-Iggy down the path, me and Tim waited for them and I distracted them while Tim whacked them both with a duck stone, he knocked them both unconscious, then we took off before the police came." "What about you, how did you go on?" Tim asked Rebecca. "Well, I had a visit from the police before I came out just now, they told me that the two men are in hospital, one is still unconscious, but they are both under arrest." "The police said the men were armed, one with a gun the other with a knife, they also had a quantity of drugs on them." "The police asked if I knew how they came to be unconscious, I told them I had no idea, which was the truth." "They also said they had been watching these two for some time, hoping they could catch them in possession of drugs, and when they found them unconscious and armed, they thought it was their birthday." The three friends arrived at the grove and checked around to see if anything had been disturbed. Then they sat on one of the logs to talk. Hotpot was deep in thought, staring into space. "What's the matter with you?" Tim asked him. "I was just thinking about those two thugs being armed with a gun and a knife and what could have happened to us," said Hotpot. Tim laughed, "don't dwell on what might have been," he said, "you did a brilliant job, and I'm proud of you, and everything turned out good, so be happy." "Anyway," said Tim, "it wasn't just us; it was mainly Vortan, and we wouldn't be doing any of this without him, would we?" "Absolutely not," said hotpot, "without his strength and ability supporting us, I wouldn't say boo to a goose." "What's more, said Hotpot, I could never have imagined that you would change like you have, since Vortan appeared." "I'm glad he did appear," said Tim, "and I think we have all changed, and for the better, don't you agree?" he asked. "We have all changed," said Rebecca, "and we have all benefited from Vortan's arrival, haven't we?" "Maybe," said Hotpot, "but all this violence is a bit much isn't it?" "You're right," said Tim, "Vortan is violent, but you must understand, he is a warrior, he was brought up fighting, he had to fight in order to survive, and what's more he died fighting." "Another thing, there has always been violence, we have all suffered from violence in one way or another, but since we met Vortan we have been able to stand up to it, and not just be victims, so Vortan has taught us to be stronger people, and not just punch-bags." Then Tim laughed. "What are you laughing at?" asked Hotpot. "Could you imagine, just a few weeks ago, Bull-Iggy coming to us and asking sincerely for our help in that way?" said Tim. "Not really," said Hotpot, "I suppose you're right." he admitted, "but when I think about me jumping out to scare them two thugs, and them being armed with guns and knives, it makes me shudder." They all had to laugh about that, even though it wasn't that funny.

"Vortan hasn't just been violent," commented Rebecca, "he has given all of us a new lease of life, and we have all become stronger, fitter, and happier, haven't we?" "I suppose so agreed," Hotpot, "anyway, I'm going to have a climb in the trees, who's coming?" "Just a minute," said Rebecca, as she took a small brown paper bag from her shoulder bag, she walked over to the stone altar and took the contents from the bag and placed them on the slab, an apple an orange and a banana. "It's just an offering to the ancient gods for being so kind and looking after us." Tim smiled, Hotpot pulled a funny screwed up face and went to climb some trees. Tim sat on one of the logs and watched Rebecca as she placed the fruit on the altar, then put her hands together and raised her head, saying a quiet prayer. Tim looked at Rebecca and couldn't help reflecting on the scene he had witnessed in Vortan's memory, when he saw Vortan's mother, the tribal priestess (Merva) conducting a ceremony at that very altar. Tim felt strange watching Rebecca stood there praying to the same gods, she was tall and had beautiful long black hair, just like Merva. He felt a shiver run down his spine as he sat watching. Rebecca turned and saw Tim looking at her so intently. "What?" she said, "What are you looking at?" Tim smiled and shook his head. "You wouldn't believe me if I told you." He spoke. "Try me," she said. Tim explained how he had visualised Vortan's memories of an event in his life and how it ended in a ceremony in this grove, presided over by Merva, the high priestess, and how watching her now, looked so much like Merva. Rebecca smiled, she was incredibly pleased to be compared to Merva even though she didn't know anything about those times or the kind of ceremonies that took place. Tim explained that the ceremony he saw was rather gruesome and involved offerings to the gods of human heads. Rebecca cringed at this idea, but she was still interested in learning more about the people who used to live here especially Vortan's family.

Tim agreed, with Vortan's help that he would try and tell her as much as he could about Vortan's family and their Celtic tribal life estimated to be about, Seven Hundred BC. Rebecca said she would get some history books from the library and do some studying on Celtic history. Tim thought that would be a good idea, but could she get that monkey out of the trees and get him to learn something. Rebecca laughed, "Hotpot just loves climbing, doesn't he?" she said. "He's only small but he's very fit and agile, I don't think he'll be interested in reading any books though, but we can try." Tim laughed, "I think you're right, getting Hotpot to read history books could be difficult, but never mind, he's happy in the trees."

CHAPTER TWENTY-ONE

VORTAN'S TREASURE

Tim had brought his metal detector with him and decided to have a search in the woods around the outside of the grove. Rebecca stayed in the grove by the altar trying to immerse herself in the atmosphere of ancient rituals, while Hotpot seemed to be determined to climb every tree in the woods. After about half an hour or so, having had no success with his metal detector, Tim decided to go back into the grove, when Vortan spoke to him, "what are you looking for Tim?" he asked. "Nothing in particular," said Tim, "but I would like to find some interesting artefacts, perhaps from your time, but it was a long time ago and very few items have survived from that era." Vortan spoke again. "What kind of things would you like?" he said. "Something interesting, like a spear head or anything in reasonable condition that can be identified properly," said Tim. "I know where we can find some nice things," said Vortan. "Really?" asked Tim. "What kind of things?" "Well, we could go and look for my ceremonial things, my gold handled sword, my gold torque and armlets, and whatever else is left of our tribal treasures." Said Vortan. "Are you joking?" laughed Tim. "No, I'm not joking," said Vortan, "Wouldn't you like to find things like that?" "Of course, I would like to find things like that," said Tim, "that would be wonderful, a dream come true, but surely those things would be well gone by now, wouldn't they?" "I doubt it," said Vortan, they were well hidden." "But do you know where they were hidden?" "Of course, I know where they were hidden, it was me that hid them there, they are in the grove." Tim was getting quite excited by the thought of finding Vortan's treasures, but he knew that he had searched all over the grove and all that he had found was Vortan's bronze axe. Not that he would belittle that very important find or that very important day in his life, for it had been that day, and that find that had changed his life forever, and for the good.

"I have searched all over the grove and I have found only your axe." Said Tim. "If they were so badly hidden, the Cunai would have found them, but they were hidden better than that," said Vortan. "Come," said Vortan, "let's go and see if we can find some treasure." "Wait," said Tim, hesitating. "We must go and speak to Mr and Mrs Bickerstaff and get their permission, if there is something valuable here, it really belongs to them, because they own the land hear, and anything on it belongs to them. Vortan became quite incensed by this. "Tim," he said, "these things belong to me and my people, as does the land." "Not anymore," said Tim, "unfortunately, your people have gone, and the land has been passed on to other people, as difficult as it may be, we have to accept that don't we?" asked Tim. Vortan was silent. "Speak to me," said Tim, "why have you gone quiet?" Eventually Vortan spoke. "If we are not allowed to own our own treasures, then they can stay where they are, then nobody can have them." He was obviously upset that he couldn't have his own property. Tim tried to console him. "Let's just go and see Mr and Mrs Bickerstaff and talk to them, they are really nice people, and if they are not agreeable, we can just leave those things where they are, and not even look for them." "OK," said Vortan. "I'll go along with you for now, "but I'm beginning to have less and less respect for these ridiculous laws." Tim called to Hotpot and Rebecca to tell them he was going over to the farmhouse to speak to Mr and Mrs Bickerstaff for a few minutes, they seemed to be happy doing what they were doing.

Tim knocked on the farmhouse door, and was greeted by Mrs Bickerstaff, "Hello Tim, how are you today?" she asked as she gave him a hug and kiss, "I saw you and your friends playing in the grove, are you having a good time?" "Yes thanks, how are you feeling today?" "I'm fine Tim, thanks, Jack will be in shortly, and he'll be pleased to see you." "Is he OK?" asked Tim. "Yes, he's fine," she said. "Why don't you call little Sam and Rebecca over for a drink," she said. "OK," said Tim, "but I wanted to talk to you and Mr Bickerstaff about something." "Oh, that sounds serious," she said, smiling, "anyway he's heard now, so you can talk away." "Hello Tim," said Mr Bickerstaff, how are you?" "Fine thanks," said Tim, "but I would like to talk to you both about what's happened to me." "OK Tim, go ahead," said Mr Bickerstaff. Tim was rather nervous, but he thought it needed to be done, so he started to explain. "You have been so kind to me, so I feel I need to be honest and upfront with you, about the grove." He spent a few minutes telling them what had happened when he found Vortan's axe, and how Vortan materialised in front of him, and how Vortan was now part of him, and how it has all made such a difference in his life. They both looked at one another, then looked back at Tim. Mrs Bickerstaff spoke, "We know that the grove is a special place, and we know that you have a special feeling for the place." "We also know that there has been a settlement hear for a long time, and we consider ourselves the custodians of the place, we respect the memory of the people who lived here, and apart from losing our little boy James, when he was three, we've had a very happy life hear."

"Also we feel that since you turned up the place and ourselves have been blessed by your presence, so although your story is most unusual we are prepared to go along with what you have told us, but the bit about a Celtic warrior, is difficult to take." Tim thought for a moment, it was time for Vortan to show himself once again, so he turned his thoughts inward and asked Vortan to oblige. Just then, Vortan appeared, but not with his war paint on, he looked very impressive with his long blonde hair and tanned skin, with a beautiful muscular body, and holding a long spear in one hand and his bronze axe in the other, he just stood there and smiled at the farmer and his wife. They both sat watching with their mouths wide open. "This is Vortan," said Tim. "Does he speak?" asked Mrs Bickerstaff nervously. "Yes," said Tim, "but I don't think you would understand him, the language is ancient, and I couldn't understand a word." Just then Vortan disappeared. "Where's he gone?" asked Jack. "He's inside me," said Tim, "he is now part of me, he says he has always been a part of me, but just a small part of him and when I released the rest of his spirit from the axe, then he was able to join with me completely." "Which means I am now Tim and Vortan combined, I'm afraid it's all very confusing." "He communicates with my mind directly, which doesn't require language." Mr and Mrs Bickerstaff sat completely dumfounded, but they had little choice but to believe what had been there before them. They had a lot of questions but were too dumbstruck to say anything. Tim laughed and walked over to them both sat on the couch and took hold their hands. "It's alright," said Tim, Vortan is our friend, he just wants to help." "Does he know anything about farming?" joked Jack, struggling to speak. Tim laughed, "I doubt it, he was a famous warrior, he spent his life fighting, to defend his people, but if you need any help with the farm I will gladly help, and that includes Vortan, and I'm sure Hotpot and Rebecca would love to help also."

"Talking about Hotpot and Rebecca, I'd better go and get them, they'll think I've gone home without them." Mr and Mrs Bickerstaff thanked Tim for being honest with them, saying. It must have been difficult for him. They said they would talk some more in a day or so, in the meantime take care and give their regards to his mother. Tim walked the short distance from the farmhouse to the grove, thinking about Mr and Mrs Bickerstaff. He'd completely forgotten why he went to see them in the first place, which was to ask about searching for Vortan's treasure. Vortan spoke to Tim and told him to leave it where it is for now. Tim agreed, he collected Rebecca and hotpot and headed home.

On the way home Rebecca talked about the grove and how she felt a strange feeling when she was in there, she said she felt an extraordinarily strong attraction to the place, as if there was something drawing her there. "What do you think that could be?" She asked Tim. "Perhaps it's the ancient gods, or goddesses, or perhaps it's the spirit of Vortan's mother, 'Merva,' said Tim. "She was an immensely powerful Celtic priestess, who practiced ancient magic, she was the leader of the 'Vanai Tribe' although Vortan's father 'Etain' and then after his father's death Vortan, were supposed to be the tribal leaders." "Merva was the real leader; she came from a long line of Celtic priests and priestesses, she was originally from Wales, and nobody did anything in that tribe without her say so." "She was, according to Vortan, a very powerful magician, and people came from great distances to consult with her." "Tribal leaders and even kings, came to seek her advice, she was a woman of great wisdom, and commanded a great deal of respect." "Above all, she was considered the greatest healer in the land, and Vortan says her healing powers were particularly special." "Also Vortan has inherited some of her healing powers," said Tim, "both myself and my mother have benefited from these abilities, firstly, when I got into that fight with Bull-Iggy and ended up with some bad cuts and bruises, but within a couple of hours Vortan made them completely heal, with all sign of the injuries disappearing, and then my mother's injuries were quite serious, and Vortan helped her through that very difficult time and she made a miraculous recovery, and she knew it was down to Vortan, even though she had been unconscious at the time."

"So, if you feel drawn to the grove, like that, perhaps you are being drawn by the spirit of Merva, or maybe it's the ancient gods or goddesses that are drawing you, either way you should feel honoured," said Tim. "There is also the business of your eyesight, which dramatically improved over night, after you first came to the grove." "Perhaps you have been chosen to continue Merva's work as a healer," suggested Tim. "Do you think so?" said Rebecca. "It would be brilliant, but it sounds a bit farfetched," she said. Hotpot laughed, "It would be a bit of a change from us going around putting people in hospital, wouldn't it?" he said jokingly. They all laughed. "Well," said Tim, "we won't bother them, if they don't bother us!" It sounded like Vortan's thinking. "What about me" said Hotpot, joking, "I don't feel drawn to anything, does that make me an outsider?" Tim laughed, "Don't be ridiculous," he said, "You enjoy yourself as much as anybody in the grove, you know you do." "I do," said hotpot. "I love the trees and the flowers, and I really love climbing, but I don't know anything about being drawn to the place!" "I just like us all being together and having fun," he said. Hotpot was always very cheerful and light-hearted, but never very deep thinking. "Don't tell me you don't feel drawn to the trees," said Tim, "you know very well you do," "I never thought about that," said Hotpot.

He liked to keep life very simple. Tim mentioned that Mr Bickerstaff could do with some help on the farm, and that he had volunteered them both and himself when needed." "Thanks," said Hotpot, "that's just what we needed." Rebecca laughed, "I'd love to help," she said, "they're such lovely people, aren't they?" "OK then," said Tim, "that's settled, we're all going to help on the farm, aren't we?" "OK," Hotpot and Rebecca both agreed. "Actually," said Tim, I think the Bickerstaff's are just pleased to have us around, perhaps they're a bit lonely, or they miss their little boy who died a long time ago." Whatever the reason they all agreed that they would help whenever they were needed. The three friends all went home in a happy mood.

CHAPTER TWENTY-TWO

GOOD NEWS FOR TINA

When Tim arrived home his mother was sat waiting for him, she had some news, "I've been given my old job back at the library," she said excitedly. She had worked as a librarian for years but being married to Duncan had taken its toll, like facial injuries and regular visits to hospital. She was forced to give up her job three years since, but today she had been to see her old boss who had offered her, her old job back. She was extremely excited, that her life was beginning to turn around after years of misery at the hands of her brutal monstrous husband. Tim was so pleased for his mother as he gave her a big hug, "When are you starting back?" he asked. "Next Monday," said Tina, "that is, if the doctor thinks I'm fit enough, I have to go and see him tomorrow." "You'll be fine," said Tim, "you look wonderful, especially since that picnic, your eyes sparkle, you're bruises have all disappeared, in fact I've never seen you looking so fit and healthy." "I feel good," she said, "so let's hope the doctor thinks I'll be fit to work." "Would you like me to come to the doctors with you?" asked Tim. "No," said Tina, "you've lost enough time off school recently, I want you to do well with your studies, which would make me happy." "OK," said Tim, if that's what you want, I'll go to school."

CHAPTER TWENTY-THREE

POLICE AT SCHOOL

Tim met Rebecca and Hotpot on the way to school, they both seemed to be in a happy mood as they rode the bus downtown. Tim was telling his friends about his mother's news when he was interrupted, it was Bull-Higgy, he had just boarded the bus and stepped along the isle until he got to where Tim and hotpot were sitting, Rebecca was in the seat behind. "What now?" said Tim, as he looked up at the bull. "I want to thank you for your help." "Shush," gestured Tim, "Sorry," whispered the bull, but you all did me a big favour and I'm so grateful, and I promise I'll never forget what you all did for me. "OK," said Tim "but it's important that you don't tell anyone, 'Ever' what really happened, do you understand that?" "Yes," said the bull, "I understand." "Good," said Tim. They got off the bus and walked up the road to school. When they arrived in the school yard, they noticed that there were two police cars outside the office. Tim turned to his friends and impressed upon them that they must not tell the police what really happened. They all agreed. The police were questioning pupils all day about what had happened the day before, but without much success. Rebecca did own up to being the person who had phoned in the first place, but she convinced them that she knew nothing else about what was going on, or what happened afterwards. She simply said she saw two nasty looking men chasing a boy down the woodland path, so she thought she should call the police. She asked if she was in trouble for calling them. The police assured her she had done the right thing. Tim and Hotpot just acted dumb about the whole thing. Hotpot looked at Tim as they walked down the corridor away from the interview room. "We're getting good at telling lies, aren't we? He spoke. Tim just laughed as he put his arm around him. "If we tell them that we, did it and we were helped by a two thousand seven-hundred-year-old Celtic warrior, they'd put us in a mental home, wouldn't they? So, we don't really have a choice, do we?" he said. "OK," laughed Hotpot. "I suppose you're right." It was Friday, and Tim, Hotpot and Rebecca arranged to go and do some work in the grove over the weekend.

Tim arrived home to find his mother in good spirits because she had been given all clear by the doctor, so she could start back at work on Monday, she was delighted and gave Tim a big hug as she told him her happy news. Tim asked his mother if it would be all right for him to go with Rebecca and Hotpot to the grove at weekend and do some work. "Of course it's alright, but please don't make a nuisance of yourselves with the Bickerstaff, will you?" said Tina. "OK," said Tim. "There is something else I would like to ask you about, because I don't know what to do about it," he said. "Just ask," said Tina. "Well said," Tim,

Vortan tells me he can show me where his treasures are hidden, but when I told him that we can't just dig things up and keep them, he said then we will leave them where they are, he says that if we can't have our own things, then nobody else will have them."

"That's difficult," said Tina, "because you are supposed to hand over any valuables to the authorities, who will then evaluate them and decide where they will go, like perhaps the British museum, they would then decide how much to pay the finder." "That doesn't seem fair from Vortan's point of view, does it, seeing as they belong to him anyway?" said Tim. "No, it doesn't," replied Tina. But you can't tell people that Vortan lives in you, can you, they would think you'd gone mad, wouldn't they?" "Of course not," said Tim, "so what shall we do?" Tina thought seriously for a moment then replied, "I think Vortan has the right idea, leave them where they are for now, until we can figure out the best thing to do." There is also the matter of including the Bickerstaff's in any decision to look for treasure on their land." "Yes of course," said Tim, "I tried to speak to them about it the other day, but I got sidetracked and didn't mention it in the end," he said. Tina gave Tim a serious look, "do they know about Vortan?" she asked hesitantly. Tim nodded, "Yes," he said, "I'm sorry mum, I felt so guilty about keeping it from them as it was their land, and they had been so kind to us all, it didn't seem fare on them, so I asked Vortan to make an appearance." "How did they take it?" asked Tina. "OK, I suppose, under the circumstances," replied Tim, "It's a real shock for anybody, but they took it as well as can be expected, and I'm glad I told them, because they're such good people and I don't want to be deceitful with them," he said. "You're a good boy," said Tina, "I hope you stay that way, you're right about the Bickerstaff's, I think you should be absolutely honest with them always, they deserve that." "I agree," said Tim, "I will be,"

CHAPTER TWENTY-FOUR

MERVA'S WELL AND THE OLD SETTLEMENT

Saturday morning Rebecca and Hotpot arrived at Tim's, and they all set off for the grove. As they reached the grove Tim asked the other two to start clearing any stones from the grass so they could borrow a grass cutter from Mr Bickerstaff and give the area a clean-up before winter sets in, it was late September now, and they wanted to do as much as possible before the frost and the snow and the heavy rains prevented them from doing anything. Tim knocked on the farmhouse door, it was a few minutes before Mr Bickerstaff answered. "Hello Tim, come in," he said. Tim was confused because Mr Bickerstaff seemed sad. "What's the matter?" asked a genuinely concerned Tim. "It's Mrs Bickerstaff, she's been sick for two days now and it's not like her she's never ill, I don't know what's wrong with her, she just won't get out of bed, she's normally so cheerful, I don't know what to do." "Can I go and see her?" asked Tim. "Yes," perhaps you can cheer her up, I couldn't, said Mr Bickerstaff, sadly." Tim followed Mr Bickerstaff upstairs. "Hey Mary, Tim's come to see you," said Jack. Mrs Bickerstaff sat up in bed and forced a smile just for Tim and held her hand out to Tim. Tim took hold of her hand. He had never seen her looking so sad.

"What's wrong with you?" asked Tim, very concerned. "I don't know Tim, I just feel weak, I have no energy and simply don't have the strength to get out of bed, but I don't know what it is." "I'll go and make a cup of tea," said Jack, "Are you going to stay for a few minutes Tim?" "Of course," replied Tim, "but Rebecca and Hotpot are in the grove, we wanted to borrow a grass cutter to tidy the place up before winter sets in, do you think that would be alright?" "No problem," said Mr Bickerstaff, I've phoned for the doctor, so if you stay with Mary for a while I will go and cut the grass for you, it will only take a few minutes, just listen out for the doctor, and I'll be back soon." "Thanks." Said Tim. Just then Tim felt Vortan staring in his head. "What is it?" he asked Vortan, silently. "Put your hand on her forehead," said Vortan. "What for?" asked Tim silently. "We can give her some energy, just do it." Said Vortan, "Now." Tim let go of Mary's hand and nervously placed it on her forehead. As he did so he felt the strangest feeling, like a tingling through his hand just like electricity. He noticed Mary was smiling and looking much more relaxed. "That feels wonderful Tim, how do you do that?" she asked. "It's not me it's Vortan," replied Tim hesitantly. Tim left his hand there for a minute or so, then much to his amazement, Mary said to Tim, "go and tell Jack, I'll make the tea, he can go and cut the grass for you, I feel fine now!" Tim looked at

Mrs Bickerstaff in disbelief, one minute she looked really ill, the next minute she's jumping out of bed full of energy, her eyes sparkling. "Tell Vortan, thanks very much, I don't know how he did it, but it really works, for the last few days I've felt so bad, and now I feel wonderful.

Tim went downstairs where Mr Bickerstaff was making a pot of tea. Tim told him what Mrs Bickerstaff had said. He looked at Tim in disbelief. "Are you kidding me?" he said. Just then, Mrs Bickerstaff came into the kitchen, dressed and looking full of energy. Back to her usual cheerful self. Mr Bickerstaff just stood there looking at her, shaking his head. "I'll do that, she said, you go and do Tim's little job for him, and I'll cook us a meal, I feel hungry." "How did that happen?" said Jack, with tears in his eyes. "Ask Tim, he says it was his strange friend Vortan, but all I know is that Tim put his hand on my forehead, and it filled me with energy, and I feel fine now." she said. Tim felt Vortan prompting him, "Tell her to rest Tim," he said, "there's still something wrong with her, which we can help with later but for now she should rest because the flood of energy she feels at the moment won't last." Tim took hold of Mrs Bickerstaff's hand. "Please come and sit down, you need to rest," he said, "I'll bring the tea, and we can talk." "But I feel fine," she said. "I know you do, but Vortan says you should rest because the way you feel right now won't last, he says that you have a health problem and he will try and help you with it but for now you should just rest and take it easy for a while," said Tim. "Very well," I'll go and sit in the living room, you bring the tea, and we'll have a talk," she said. Tim and Mrs Bickerstaff sat chatting in the living room, until Mr Bickerstaff came back from the grove. "How are you feeling now, my love?" asked Jack.

"I'm fine," said Mary, "but Vortan says I have to rest so I'm resting." "Good," said Jack, that's a good idea." Just then the doctor arrived so Tim said he would go to the grove and see how Hotpot and Rebecca were going on. "Thanks Tim," said Mrs Bickerstaff, "and thank Vortan for me." Tim nodded as he left and went across to the grove.

Hotpot and Rebecca had been busy, and the place was looking really good with all the grass cut short and the blossoms on the trees all around the edge of the grove looking colourful. It was a beautiful sight, and the smell of the newly cut grass was rich, also the place was alive with the sound of birds singing all around the edge of the grove. There was even a family of red squirrels playing in the trees at one end of the grove. Tim smiled as he reflected on the way the place used to be when he first came here with his metal detector.

There were no birds singing there then, it was a strange and gloomy place. "Well, what do you think?" asked Rebecca, "do you like the place now?" "It's wonderful," said Tim, "and I'm sorry I was so long, Mrs Bickerstaff has been ill, and I thought I might be able to help, but I am so pleased with the job you've both done here." "Vortan says that the gods are smiling on us and the grove, he says that in the old days the grove was special and sacred, but it was rather gloomy." "But now the grove is full of flowers and blossoms and birds singing in the place, even animals playing in there, it never happened before!" "It seems that the gods have blessed us and changed the grove from a place of worship and gruesome sights, into a place of fun and beauty," said Tim. "Well, I think it's beautiful hear," said Rebecca, "and when I'm in hear I feel special and particularly happy, and I'm sure Hotpot loves it here also, don't you?" she said as she turned to Hotpot. "Of course I do, I've never been so happy in my life," said Hotpot. "But I do think we should do some work in the rest of the woods, some of the trees need attention, and some brambles need to be cleared, and the stream needs clearing of blockages in places." Tim and Rebecca both looked at Hotpot in surprise. "You're very fond of the woods, aren't you?" Rebecca said to Hotpot. "Well, aren't you?" said Hotpot. "Yes," said Rebecca, "I am, but I particularly love the grove, were as you like all the woods, don't you?" "Yes, you're right," said Hotpot, "I do like all the woods, I love the trees, they're my friends," he said. Tim and Rebecca both laughed. "We'll have to make hotpot the keeper of the trees," said Tim. "That's a good idea," said Rebecca. Hotpot smiled smugly.

Tim turned his thoughts to Vortan and asked him what he thought was wrong with Mrs Bickerstaff. "I'm not sure," said Vortan, "but I think we can help her. "How do we do that?" asked Tim. "Well, my mother was a great healer and she taught me a lot of her skills, and I'm sure we can heal her if we put our minds to it." Said Vortan. "What can I do to help?" asked Tim. Vortan thought for a moment, then replied. "Over in our settlement there was a sacred well, if we could recover it, we could call on the gods to restore the healing powers that it's waters once possessed," Rebecca looked at Tim sat on one of the logs, deep in thought. "You look as if you're somewhere else, miles away," she said, quizzically, what are you thinking?" she asked. "Sorry?" said Tim, "I was asking Vortan about Mrs Bickerstaff's illness and if there was anything we could do to help." "And what did he say?" asked Rebecca. "He said we should try and find the sacred well in the old settlement and bring it back into use, then ask the old gods to restore the healing powers of the waters," said Tim. "Where's the old settlement?" asked Hotpot, "and how would we know where to look for the well?" "I know where the settlement is," said Tim," it's just over there about a hundred yards away, where that raised bank is." "How do you know that?" asked Hotpot. "Vortan showed me in a vision," replied Tim, There used to be a deep ditch all the way around with an earth wall and a bridge to a gateway, but the bridge has gone and the deep ditch has been re-rooted, it's just down one side now, but you can still see the earth wall and where the entrance used to be." "Let's go and have a look then," said Rebecca excitedly. "OK," said Tim, "Come on." They all set off running, following Tim, along the pathway and over the bridge from the grove and along the brook until they came to where the brook turned sharp right, then just a few yards further. In the old days the brook had gone straight on as well as turning right, it had encircled the settlement completely and was much deeper than now, and it was flowing with deep water then.

As they approached the place where the old settlement used to be Tim felt a strange shiver as he remembered the vision of when he travelled there with Vortan, after chasing and killing the Cunai warriors, then carrying their decapitated heads over the bridge and through the gateway into the compound. The thought of that vision made Tim stop in his tracks before they reached where the bridge used to be. "What is it?" said Rebecca. "What's up?" "It's alright," said Tim, as he walked through the dry ditch where the bridge used to be, "Come on," he said as he climbed the far bank and through what used to be the gateway, there was still an earth wall, but not as high as it used to be, it was all overgrown with bushes and nettles, even some trees growing from it. As they passed through what had been the gateway, they could see it was like a compound, oval shaped, it was all overgrown now, but Tim could see it as it used to be as it was in the vision. He felt a strange staring in his stomach as he looked around the area, he could almost see the children running to greet the warriors and surrounding the old chief, Vortan's father, and then the appearance of Vortan's mother, Merva in her white robe with her long flowing jet black hair.

"Are you alright Tim?" asked Rebecca, "You look really strange," she said. "I'm OK," said Tim, pulling himself together. They all looked around the compound, it was overgrown but was still a high platform overlooking the surrounding land. "Where are we going to look for the well?" asked Hotpot. "I think we'll leave that to Vortan," said Tim. He then turned to Vortan and enquired where he thought the well was located. "Over in that corner, it was behind the smith's hut," said Vortan, "When we were small children we used to sit and watch the smith making tools and weapons, he always had a very hot fire and in the winter the children would gather round to keep warm, and watch as the sparks were flying as the smith beat the metal into shape." "The smith was called Irkel, he wasn't very tall, but he was very strong, he had a son called Lew and a daughter called Semper, Irkel was a friendly man, always smiling and joking with the children." Tim led the others to the corner where Vortan indicated. They searched but there didn't appear to be any sign of a well. Vortan guided Tim where he remembered the spot where the well was. They all searched through the weeds and grass until they came to a square patch of earth that seemed slightly different, they scraped the soil away and found a large sandstone slab just a few inches below the surface, it was much too heavy for them to move. "We'll have to ask Mr Bickerstaff if he will move it for us," said Tim.

Rebecca and Hotpot cleared the weeds and grass from all around the stone while Tim went across to the farmhouse. "Come on in Tim," called Mr Bickerstaff, "What did the doctor have to say?" asked Tim. "He couldn't find anything wrong with Mary; in fact, I don't think he was very pleased that we'd called him out, but if he'd have seen her before you came he would probably have sent her to hospital; anyway she's gone to bed for now to rest. Said Jack "Good," said Tim. "There's something Vortan wants us to do in order to try and help Mrs Bickerstaff!" "Oh," said Jack, "What's that?" Tim explained what Vortan had said about the waters from the well, and how he thinks they could help Mrs Bickerstaff. "Where's the well?" asked Jack. "I think we've found it, with Vortan's help!" said Tim, "but we need you to come and help us." "OK," said jack, "let's go and see what you've found."

He went with Tim to the raised area, which was only sixty or seventy yards from the farmhouse. Rebecca and Hotpot were there waiting; having cleared all around the stone slab. Jack looked at the slab quizzically. "Does Vortan reckon that there's a well under there?" "Not just a well!" said Tim, "but a very special, sacred well, a well with special healing powers, and Vortan says that the waters could be very beneficial to Mrs Bickerstaff." "His mother was (Merva) a priestess and a great healer and he wants us to clear the well and make it good again, he believes that the spirit of Merva will still heal anyone who drinks the water!" Mr Bickerstaff stared at the stone slab, deep in thought for a few moments. "I'll go and get the tractor and put the forks on it and see if we can lift the slab off to see what's under there.

When Jack returned with the tractor, they set about lifting the stone slab. They were all eager to see what lay under it. The tractor struggled to make any movement; the slab must have weighed at least two tons, plus the suction of the soil was making it very heavy, but eventually, with a lot of shaking and straining of the tractor the slab sprung loose and once free of the suction started to lift much easier. Jack backed the tractor away, clearing the slab from where it had been lying for perhaps hundreds of years. Jack jumped down from the tractor and all four peered down what seemed to be a bottomless hole. Jack took a rope from the tractor and tied a heavy stone on one end, then lowered it down the hole until the stone touched the bottom. "It's quite deep!" said Jack, but it will have to be cleaned and we'll have to get the water analyzed before it can be used." "OK," said Tim, "but how long will it take to do all that?" "I don't know," said Jack, "but I'll go on Monday and get it all done as soon as possible." "Thanks," said Tim. "You're welcome," said Jack, "but you know, if this well water proves to be good and beneficial for people, perhaps we could sell it also; what do you think about that?" asked Jack. "Sounds like a good idea to me, said Tim. "It might even make the farm profitable for a change, said Jack. "What do you mean?" said Tim, seriously. "Well, not many farms make money nowadays," said Jack, "and sadly, this one hasn't been profitable for three years now, so anything that could help, would be welcome." Tim and his two friends were surprised to hear this sad news and vowed that if there was anything they could do, they would gladly help. "Thanks," said Jack, "I appreciate your offer, and if this well proves to be our saviour, I'll make sure that you all get some benefit from the venture." Tim and his two friends were quite moved by Mr Bickerstaff's honesty and his kindness. He was a kind and gentle man they thought.

Sunday morning and the three friends all agreed to go and tidy up the area around the well which had originally been the Vanai settlement. It was a raised area, like a plateau about sixty or seventy yards long by fifty yards wide, it was oval shaped, with a raised earthen bank all around. The bank was not very high now in most places, but it had obviously been about nine or ten feet high originally as there were a few places where the bank was still that height. The gateway was still quite obvious but was not very imposing now. Tim had done a rough drawing of the settlement as he had remembered it from his vision and then enlisted the help of Vortan when he couldn't remember any more, there were about twenty huts of various sizes around the edge of the compound and a large hut, much bigger than any of the others in the centre. Tim had also included the location of the well in his drawing with a circle of stones. Hotpot and Rebecca were fascinated looking at the drawing on the way to the farm. When the three friends arrived, Mr Bickerstaff was already there working, he was sat on his grass cuter and had already cut half of the area. He gave a wave to Tim and the others as they approached. Mr Bickerstaff shut the grass cutter off and climbed down. "Hi kids, how are you? I've started to tidy the place up a bit, what do you think?" "That's great," said Tim, "it's looking good, already." "How is Mrs Bickerstaff this morning?" "She's a bit miserable," said Jack, "I think she'd be pleased if you could go and spend a few minutes with her, she's always happy to see you, you know." "OK," said Tim, "but my mother is coming along, to spend some time with her in a little while, I hope that's alright?" "That's fine!" said Jack.

While Rebecca and Hotpot helped Mr Bickerstaff to tidy up the old settlement Tim jogged across to the farmhouse and knocked on the door. There was no answer, so Tim opened the door and went in. Mrs Bickerstaff was dozing on the couch in the living room. She opened her eyes as Tim came in the room. "Hello sweetheart," she said as she held out her hand, and gestured to Tim to come and sit with her on the couch. "How are you today?" asked Tim. "I could do with some of that magic that Vortan does, do you think you could ask for his help?" "No need!" said Tim, "he hears you." With that Tim held out his right hand and placed it on Mary's forehead. She closed her eyes and lay her head back on the pillow smiling. Tim could feel the tingling as the energy passed through his hand. After a couple of minutes Tim took his hand away as Mary opened her eyes. "Thank you, I feel better already!" she said as she gave Tim a hug. "I don't know how you do that, but it really works, please thank Vortan for me." "No need," said Tim, he hears you!" "He also says that you need a more permanent cure, which is why we're trying to restore the old well, he says that it's waters can have miraculous healing powers, or at least they used to have in his time!" "He wants us to restore the well and ask the ancient gods to restore the healing properties of the waters, he also wants to appeal to the spirit of Merva, his mother, to use her healing for you!"

Mary was quite overwhelmed by all this talk of ancient gods and the spirit of Merva. Tim was a little upset when he saw tears running down Mary's cheeks. "Are you alright?" asked Tim as he took hold of her hand again. "I'm fine!" replied Mary, "I'm just not used to all this attention, especially not from ancient gods or mystic priestesses, it's a lot to take in you know!" Tim laughed, "well it's Vortan's idea, not mine and he seems to know what he's talking about, but we must be cautious because we don't know if the gods, or Merva will respond yet, they have been ignored for such a long time now, we don't know how our efforts will be received." Mary nodded her head, as she squeezed Tim's hand. "Vortan is a good man, with a warm heart!" she said. Tim laughed again, "Vortan was a famous warrior who killed over fifty warriors in his time, I don't imagine those people would have thought he was such a good man with a warm heart, would they?" he said jokingly. "Well tell him I'm grateful for all his efforts to help me and tell him also that the difference he has already made to our lives is very much appreciated," she said. "He hears you!" said Tim. Just then there was a knock on the front door. "That'll be my mother," said Tim, "she wanted to come and see if there was anything she could do for you; if not she can just sit and have a chat for a while," "Oh, that's kind of her, tell her to come in." Tim answered the door and showed his mother into the living room. "Hello Tina, come and sit down and tell me all about your new job," said Mrs Bickerstaff. "Never mind that; how are you doing?" said Tina, "Tim tells me you've been poorly, what's the problem?" Tim decided to remove himself from all this woman talk. "I'll go and see how the others are getting on with the well," he said, as he turned to Mrs Bickerstaff, "perhaps you could explain to my mother what we're trying to do with the well." "OK," said Mary, "we'll see you later."

When Tim arrived back at the old settlement he was delighted to see that they had cut all the grass and weeds from around whole clearing and all three were collecting sandstone blocks to put around the well, they had also removed the large sandstone slab that had been covering the well. "You've been working hard, haven't you?" said Tim. "What do you think?" Said Hotpot, holding both his clenched fists in the air, triumphantly, "are we brilliant or what?" "You're brilliant!" said Tim laughing out loud. "The place is looking really good, I do hope the gods approve," he said deep in thought.

It took most of the next week to have the water from the well analyzed, but when the results came back it was good news, There were no impurities in the water, though there were a couple of high mineral counts, but nothing harmful, and Mr Bickerstaff put in all the necessary paperwork to extract water and sell it. The next thing was to employ a drilling firm to sink a pipe and fit a pump.

CHAPTER TWENTY-FIVE

MEETING MERVA AND BLESSING THE WELL

In the meantime, with Vortan's suggestion, they all gathered at the well on Saturday evening at dusk, Mr and Mrs Bickerstaff, Tim and his mother Tina, Rebecca and Hotpot. Each one carrying a lit candle, Tim said Vortan had given him instructions and he was to explain to the others what he wanted them to do, he wanted them all, silently to ask the ancient gods and in particular Merva, to bless the sacred well and restore its healing powers. He also said that he was going to separate himself from Tim, just for a little while and that they were not to be alarmed.

Vortan promptly materialized and gestured to the others to place their candles on the wall of the well and then hold hands around the well, he took his place between Tim and Rebecca as they all closed their eyes in deep contemplation. They were all praying silently when they heard Vortan chanting out loud. They could hear him easily, but they couldn't understand a word he was chanting, it was completely unlike anything they had heard before, except of course for Tim, he had heard the same garbled tongue when he first met Vortan, but he still didn't understand a word of it.

Then a moment of silence, followed by a loud gesture from Vortan which coursed everyone to open their eyes. Most of them wished they hadn't opened their eyes, for stood in front of them close to the well was a figure of a tall woman dressed all in white, she had long shiny black hair down to her waist. She spoke to Vortan in their strange language and smiled as he answered her with tears in his eyes. Tim recognized her from his earlier vision, it was Merva, Vortan's mother.

At this point they all let go of each other's hands, primarily so they could step back, but not one of the party took their eyes off Merva. She was the most impressive of women, although she wasn't a young woman, she was the most beautiful woman that they had ever seen, she had very distinctive features, dark eyes, slender nose, a high forehead and beautiful white teeth. Merva cast her eyes over each of the party in turn, then moved on to the next; first Jack then his wife Mary then Tina and on to Tim, when her eyes rested on Vortan she spoke again and Vortan answered, at this point she looked back at Tim, which caused a cold shiver to run down his whole body, then passed on to Hotpot and last of all she looked long and hard at Rebecca. The whole party was transfixed by the presence of Merva. Hotpot would have run away but his legs wouldn't work, Rebecca was more curious than frightened, Tim didn't know what to think but his confusion was relieved when

Merva walked around the inside of the circle and stood in front of him and smiled as she reached out with both hands and gently cupped his face, he felt the most powerful feeling surge into his body, it was a feeling of motherly love, he felt himself smiling as he stared into her eyes. He felt like he had two mothers now. As he looked into her eyes, he had the strangest feeling that he had known her all his life, which was silly because he really hadn't.

He realized that the feeling of confusion and fear had disappeared, her smile was completely disarming and the touch of her hands on his face made him glow with the happiest feeling. She moved on to Vortan and took hold of both his hands and spoke again, her voice was very warm and gentle. Vortan nodded his head as she moved on to Hotpot. He was very nervous but seemed to relax as Merva smiled and looked into his eyes as she put her right hand on his head; he smiled back then she moved on and stood in front of Rebecca, who was not so much frightened of Merva but more in awe of her.

Merva reached out and took hold of Rebecca's hand and led her towards the well; then took both Rebecca's hands and placed them together in a praying pose, then turned herself to stand next to Rebecca in the same pose facing the well. She started praying in that strange tongue as the rest of the party watched on transfixed. When she'd finished praying she turned and stepped the few feet to stand in front of Mrs Bickerstaff, who was quite nervous; she reached out and placed her right hand gently on Mary's stomach and quietly spoke a few strange words, then she turned and took Rebecca back to her original place in the circle and then went and stood in front of Jack and held out both her hands. Jack felt compelled to place his hands in hers, he felt a tingle run through his whole body as Merva smiled at him. Then she moved on to Tina, took hold of her hands, looked deep into eyes and leaned forward and kissed her gently on the forehead. Then stepped back and assumed a place between Tim and Vortan; gestured to the rest of the party to hold hands once again. As they all held hands around the well once more Merva said one more prayer before disappearing out of sight.

The party blinked and shook their heads as they tried to take in what had just taken place, it took a few minutes before they realised that Vortan had also disappeared. "Wow!" said Hotpot, "that was 'Mega,' the strangest thing I have ever seen!" "But what did it all mean, really." Tina gave Tim a hug, "are you OK?" she said. "I'm fine," said Tim. "What was all that about?" asked Mr Bickerstaff. Tim seemed to have a warm glow of satisfaction as he explained. "That was Merva, Vortan's mother, and she came in response to our prayers, and her prayers were asking the ancient gods to bless the well and restore the healing power to the waters, she also wants Rebecca to be the keeper of the well, and finally she said she was very pleased that we had brought life back to the old settlement, and especially the grove!"

Tim paused deep in thought, then continued, Vortan is telling me that if we want the water especially for healing, we should draw it from the well then take it to the grove and get Rebecca to place it on the altar and ask the gods to bless it, only then will it possess the power of healing." Rebecca was feeling very strange with all this attention and particularly with all this responsibility. Tim turned to Mrs Bickerstaff, "Vortan is telling me that his mother, Merva, says that you should drink some blessed water every day, she also said that in future she will be watching over all of us as if we were her own family!" The whole party was happy and quite excited about the events of the evening. It was dark now and they all took their candles and walked in procession to the farmhouse. They all agreed to meet in the morning (Sunday) and do as Merva suggests and draw some water from the well and get Rebecca to have it blessed in the grove, they all agreed also, not to discuss what had happened with anyone else.

Sunday morning and all the friends gathered at the well, Mr Bickerstaff had brought a bucket with a long rope attached, he dropped the bucket in the well and pulled it up, the water looked crystal clear; he poured the water into a large clean bottle, one he used for his cider brew. As they took the water the short distance to the grove Mrs Bickerstaff suggested that as Rebecca was to be the keeper of the well and officiate at the blessing of the water, she should have a white robe, just like Merva's. "That's a good idea!" said Tina, "We shall make one for her this week, what do you think, Rebecca?" "Sounds good to me," said Rebecca smiling proudly. She did have a white track suit on, but it wasn't the same. Rebecca took the large bottle of water from Mr Bickerstaff and placed it on the sandstone alter, which had been dressed in two vases of beautiful flowers by Mrs Bickerstaff. She was quite embarrassed at first, but soon relaxed as she put her hands together and asked the gods to bless this water that it might serve to heal all that drank it, she then placed a bowl of fresh fruit that Tina had brought, onto the altar, as a gift to the gods. She then offered Mrs Bickerstaff a cup of the water, which she promptly drank. Then she suggested that as this was the first time, they had done this that everyone should have a drink of the water. They all agreed and queued up to in turn. The whole event reminded Tim of the vision he had of Vortan's tribe queuing up to take a drink from Merva at the ceremony of the severed heads on a moonlit night two thousand seven hundred years ago, even though it wasn't water they were drinking on that occasion it was some strange alcoholic drink. It made a little shiver run through him, but he kept quiet about it.

After relaxing in the grove for a while and laughing at Hotpot as he climbed trees as usual, they all returned to the farmhouse where Mary and Tina cooked dinner for everyone. They all had a little drink of Merva's water with the dinner of course, it had been a very satisfying day and they all felt really close to their newfound friends.

CHAPTER TWENTY-SIX

WATER FROM THE WELL

A few days later a team of drillers arrived with their equipment. Mr Bickerstaff showed them the well but instructed them not to drill just there because he wanted to preserve the well, so they drilled just outside the old settlement on the other side of the bank and what had been the ditch, which left the settlement intact. This pleased Tim and all the rest of the group. Mrs Bickerstaff had been drinking the water every day as instructed and her health was quite notably better, she was up and about every day and back to her cheerful self, she said she was never going to stop taking the water. She got together with Tim's mum, Tina and made a beautiful white robe for Rebecca and when Rebecca saw it, she was quite excited and couldn't wait to try it on. "You really look the part!" said Tim, "I think Merva would approve, you look very much like her dressed in that." Rebecca was very flattered and twirled around laughing and strutting about. They all agreed she did look like a Celtic priestess, and particularly like Merva with her beautiful long shiny black hair, she was also tall just like Merva, it was quite uncanny the resemblance, they all agreed.

Mrs Bickerstaff suggested that they could have a little ceremony from time to time in the grove and have Rebecca lead them in prayers and ask the gods and especially Merva to bless the water for healing. "That sounds like a good idea!" said Tim. The others all agreed. "It's what Merva wants anyway," said Tim, "that's what she was trying to tell you when she singled Rebecca out around the well, she wants Rebecca to represent her amongst us and be our spiritual leader, Vortan says that Merva will guide her and teach her the ways of a priestess!" They were all a little surprised to hear this, especially Rebecca, they knew that Merva had looked kindly on Rebecca, but this was a big deal, particularly for Rebecca, she was quite excited by the idea, but a little overwhelmed.

There were tears in her eyes as she paused to reflect on what this meant for her, she had never really done anything in her life that had made people notice her, until she started hanging out with Tim and Hotpot, she had tried to make herself invisible. She had been bullied at school by the in crowd and had always kept herself to herself. At home she was reasonably happy, her mother had remarried two years since and she had a new baby sister, so she had become almost invisible at home as well, so her new friendship with Tim and Hotpot and of course Tim's mum Tina and Mr and Mrs Bickerstaff, had transformed her life. The last few weeks had changed her from being shy and introverted, to a smiling, outgoing, confident young lady. Previously she had walked about with round shoulders and her head down as if she was ashamed of herself. Now she holds her head high and her shoulders back, she's dispensed with her glasses and lost more than a stone in weight. In fact she has gone from being a dowdy dull girl, to a very impressive and beautiful young lady, and indeed was attracting quite a lot of attention from people at school, not just the boys, who wanted to make her acquaintance and have a date, but also the girls who had previously ridiculed her, they also wanted to be her friend.

Rebecca just smiled and remembered when they treated her so badly, she thought how shallow they were, and was happy with her new friends, and her newfound importance as a trainee priestess, chosen by Merva.

As she stood in the living room at the Bickerstaff's, in her new white robe she felt so proud, there were tears running down her face. Mrs Bickerstaff seemed to understand, she put her arms around Rebecca and gave her a big hug. That just brought more tears, but they were tears of joy and everyone felt so pleased for her.

Mr Bickerstaff had been looking into the possibility of selling the well water and was making good progress, he needed to get certain planning permissions and licenses. He had received very encouraging responses from shops and supermarket buyers, he even had the local newspaper wanting to come and interview him about the well, and perhaps write an article about the old settlement. Things were looking up for the Bickerstaff's after years of struggling with the farm, and Tim and all the gang were so pleased for them as they were such kind and caring people, and they deserved all the luck in the world.

After a few weeks the well water was being transported by road tanker to a bottling plant and then distributed to shops and supermarkets all around the area, it was looking really good for the future of the farm and the Bickerstaff's were so pleased. Mrs Bickerstaff had been drinking the water religiously and felt quite healthy and back to her old self and what's more she was convinced that it was Merva's well water, and nothing else, that was responsible for her return to good health. She didn't need anybody to remind her of the poor state she was in before Vortan intervened, and her own doctor had done nothing whatsoever to help her situation. She was beginning to feel a strong attraction to the old ways, and to Merva and her druidic powers. She wanted to know more about her and her way of life, she decided she would ask Timothy to tell her as much as he could and then go to the library and investigate the ways of the druids and the pagan religions of Merva's period.

Meanwhile Rebecca was spending as much time as possible in the grove and trying to immerse herself in the atmosphere of the place in order to pick up on Merva's presence. She also spent a lot of time in silent prayer, asking for Merva's help, plus help from the pagan gods of Merva's time. Rebecca herself had begun to take on a quite different persona, she had become very poised and dignified, she seemed more self-assured and confident; when people spoke to her, she would answer with a knowing smile. She was becoming increasingly like Merva, in appearance and character.

The grove also was looking quite trim and manicured; Hotpot had been keeping himself busy pulling weeds and trimming the bushes and generally looking after the place and even though it was autumn time it was looking really beautiful. The birds and small animals seemed to be increasingly comfortable in the place where they had previously been reluctant to venture. The rest of the wood was also looking much better since Hotpot had been spending his time in there tidying up and clearing the blockages in the stream; he was truly fast becoming the keeper of the trees. He was also reading books to learn all about trees and wildflowers; he was quite proud of his title.

Tim meanwhile had been spending time in the library. Not just because his mother worked there, but because he wanted to learn everything, he could about the people who lived around here in Vortan's time. The Celts. He was becoming quite an expert on the subject. He was fascinated at some of the conflicting views of the so-called experts, and how the people of this period were called the 'People of the Mist', and how they had originally spread from Eastern Europe, southward through France, Spain and Italy. Then westward until they reached Britain and Ireland. Tim knew from his encounter with Vortan, and his visions of Vortan's memories that, far from being primitive cave dwellers; the Celts were very sophisticated, talented, artistic and particularly very spiritual people. He also knew that physically; the Celts were every bit as strong and athletic as people of today. He thought, any man of today would be incredibly happy with a physique like Vortan's, as he had never seen anyone with such a body. This belied the theory that people have grown bigger and stronger as time has gone on. Looking at pictures of Celtic artwork such as torques and broaches, Tin realized that the Celts were also very artistic and talented people.

He was becoming quite proud of his heritage and his earlier misgivings about being connected with Vortan had disappeared. He had now become quite honoured to be associated with a Celtic royal family and a druidic priestess. After all the misery and brutality of his earlier life, he was now feeling happy with his life. It had all changed since finding Vortan's axe and joining up with him. Tim was also feeling quite different now physically, he felt much stronger, his senses were much sharper, he held his head up higher now. He looked people strait in the eye now, something he never did before. He felt like he could jump over houses, his energy levels were much higher than before. He didn't seem to want to walk anywhere, he had to run all the time. Hotpot and Rebecca were getting annoyed with him because they couldn't keep up with his bubbling energy levels. He was also starting to pick up on some of Vortan's other powers, such as, when he approached people he was beginning to know what they were thinking, it was quite unnerving at first, but after a while he realised it could be quite useful, especially when the people concerned were not friendly.

CHAPTER TWENTY-SEVEN

TROUBLE FOR THE BICKERSTAFF'S'

One day as Tim, Hotpot and Rebecca were doing some work in the old settlement Tim noticed a car pull up at the farmhouse. He suddenly had a strange feeling of trouble in the air, he didn't know who it was, but he had this very strong feeling. "What is it, Tim?" asked Rebecca, in a genuinely concerned voice, she could see that Tim had a very strange expression on his face. "What is it?" she repeated. "Trouble!" said Tim sternly, "I don't know who that is but there's trouble ahead. "I won't ask how you know, because you've been behaving really strange lately," said Rebecca. "I'm sorry," said Tim, "I just get these very strong feelings sometimes when I meet strangers, and I don't know who that is, but they are trouble for the Bickerstaff's'!" "What can we do?" said Rebecca. "I don't know!" said Tim, "But I'll go over and see if they're all right!" Tim walked the short distance from the old settlement to the farmhouse, about two hundred yards. On the way, he turned to Vortan and asked why he was getting messages of trouble ahead. "I'm not sure," said Vortan, "but those two people have come bringing trouble for the Bickerstaff's, and what's more the trouble will involve you, so be on your guard." "Remember!" said Vortan, "These people don't know you, so you should use your intelligence and play games with them, it may help in finding out what they're up to." Tim approached the front door and knocked; he could hear shouting from inside. Mrs Bickerstaff opened the door. "Hello Tim," she said, but before she could say anymore Tim put his first finger up to his lips; "shh," he gestured. "You have trouble, haven't you?" Mary nodded, Tim moved close and spoke quietly to her. "Take me in and pretend I'm simple, tell them you're looking after me." Mary told Tim it was Jack's sister Helen, and her husband Harold, who was a notorious thug from the city.

He had spent quite a few years in prison for robbery and Violence. Tim nodded his understanding. Mary took him into the living room where the others were. "This is Tim," she said, "We're looking after him while his mother's away," she turned to Helen and Harold and spoke quietly, "He's a bit simple, so just ignore him, he doesn't understand anything." Mr Bickerstaff looked puzzled at his wife, who gave him a look, which seemed to make him understand. Tim sat down and behaved silly, twitching and giggling, so the visitors ignored him, thinking he was of no consequence. This gave Tim the opportunity to study the thug and listen to what was being said without being taken seriously. Mr Bickerstaff's sister Helen was a woman of about forty, quite good looking and well dressed. Her husband: big Harold, was rather large and heavy with dark slicked back hair and a black moustache, he was wearing a long black overcoat, and he was loud and aggressive. It seems they had heard about the Bickerstaff's' finding Merva's well and starting to sell the water. They decided that they wanted half of the money from the sale of the water. Mr Bickerstaff explained that there was no money, as he needed to borrow money from the bank to set up the operation, which he had to pay back. He also explained that Helen was entitled to nothing as she had been given all the money from their father's will while Jack was given the farm, which was much less than she received. He also pointed out that the farm had lost money for years and they had never offered to help pay the bills when he was losing money.

Mr Bickerstaff (Jack) was a big strong man, but he was never a fighter and didn't feel comfortable around his brother-in-law who was a notorious thug in the city. Big Harold ran three-night clubs and various other enterprises, most of which were rather dubious ventures. His reason for being here was that he just couldn't stand to see the Bickerstaff's' making money. He didn't like them because they were honest and hard working. He thought they were a joke, so he just had to muscle in on their good fortune. Big Harold started shouting again. "I'll be back next week, and I want that money!" Mrs Bickerstaff intervened, "You're getting nothing from us, you're nothing but a cheap thug and you're not welcome hear, either of you." She turned to Helen and said, "You should be ashamed of yourself, allowing this thug to come around hear threatening your brother!"

Meanwhile, Tim who was sat watching with great interest turned to Vortan to ask for his advice. "Sit back and leave it to me!" said Vortan. Just then, big Harold moved across the room in response to Mary's outburst, he was obviously incensed, his eyes were glaring as he approached Mary. "Don't you talk to my; ah!" His attack on Mary was cut short, by the sudden appearance of Vortan, in war mode. He stepped in front of big Harold as he approached Mary and stopped him in his tracks. Wearing war paint and wielding his bronze axe. He growled at Harold and raised the axe. Harold staggered backwards across the room, tripping over the coffee table and landing on his back on the floor. His anger had turned to abject fear as he squirmed on the floor, trying to wriggle as far away as possible from the terrifying sight in front of him. His wife, Helen let out an almighty scream, then fainted and fell back onto the couch. Harold meantime was frozen with fright, he was glaring at Vortan with eyes fixed and mouth open. Vortan stood over him growling, with his axe raised. Harold eventually managed to speak. "Who are you?" he said very nervously. This just made Vortan angrier as he leaned over and pushed his axe into Harold's neck causing him to cringe even worse. Vortan started screaming at him in his ancient tongue, at the same time he stepped back and pointed towards the door. Harold didn't understand a word of what Vortan was saying but got the gist of what he meant. He very carefully got up from the floor, never taking his eyes of Vortan, who looked as if he might attack any moment. Vortan was still pointing at the door but started screaming at Harold once again. This seemed to give Harold an added incentive to head for the door.

Having scrambled through the front door of the farmhouse, Harold tripped down the step and landed face down in front of his car. He quickly pulled himself up off the floor and struggled round to the driver's side of the car. Tim had come to the front door and burst out laughing as big Harold, the fearless gangster reversed into a sandstone wall in his panic to evacuate the premises. Harold had also forgotten to take his wife with him. Either that or he didn't fancy waiting around any longer. As Harold sped off down the private farm road Tim went back into the living room, where Helen was just beginning to recover. Vortan had retreated once more, as Helen looked up from the couch stared all around the room. She looked at her brother Jack. "What was that?" she said in a very frightened voice. Jack looked at Tim, who shook his head. "I don't know what you're talking about!" he said, "All I saw was Harold fall over the coffee table, then get up and run out." "Where is he?" she asked. "He's gone!" said Jack. "How am I going to get home?" asked Helen. "I'll take you, but I don't want you bringing that thug around here ever again, do you understand?" "I don't think you have to worry about that!" said Helen as she gathered herself together.

After Jack took his sister Helen home, Mrs Bickerstaff turned to Tim and gave him a big hug. "Tell Vortan thank you, from me, won't you?" "He hears you said Tim, he is looking after his people, just as he did all those years ago, that was his job!" said Tim. He considers you and Mr Bickerstaff part of his family now, and since you live in his old homeland, he sees it as his job to protect you, along with the rest of our group. He's just doing what he was trained to do, the thing he was really good at. "He's not just good at hurting and frightening people!" said Mary, "He's also very good at healing people, I think we owe him a lot!" she said as she gave Tim a hug. "I'd better go and see if

Hotpot and Rebecca are OK, they probably think I've gone home, I've been that long," said Tim.

He went over to the old settlement where Rebecca and Hotpot were sat on the new wall that Mr Bickerstaff had built around the well. "Where have you been?" said Rebecca, "you've been gone for ages, and we were worried about you, especially after you said there was trouble about; what's happened?"

Tim explained what had been going on with Helen and big Harold, and how Vortan had intervened and scared them away. He said it was really funny watching Harold who is a big tough gangster, squirming, and running away from Vortan, he explained how Harold had jumped into his car and reversed into the wall and wrecked his car, before taking off and leaving his wife behind. Hotpot laughed and said, "We saw him crash the car and take off, but we didn't know what had happened." "Are you alright Tim?" said Rebecca. "We were worried about you!" "I'm fine!" said Tim, let's go home."

The three friends walked home quite happy with their day, laughing as they went, thinking about what had happened with big Harold and his wife. They arranged to meet at Tim's the next morning at ten O clock and go and do some more work in the old settlement. Tim had great fun telling his mother about the events of the previous day, they had a laugh, even though it was a serious matter and potentially quite dangerous. Tina begged Tim to be incredibly careful in his dealings with people like big Harold. "OK." Said Tim, "I will."

CHAPTER TWENTY-EIGHT

REBECCA

Hotpot arrived as arranged at ten O clock, but no sign of Rebecca. They waited for a while, then decided to go round to Rebecca's to see what was keeping her, it was just a few hundred yards from Tim's. Tim was having bad feelings about something, but he couldn't figure out what it was. Rebecca answered the door. Tim and Hotpot could see that she was upset and had obviously been crying. "What's the matter?" asked Tim, very concerned. Rebecca invited them in and took them into the back room. "It's my baby sister, she's really ill, they've taken her to hospital, and I'm worried about her!" "What is it?" said Tim, "what's wrong with her?" "They're not sure," said Rebecca, "she's struggling to get her breath, they've put her on oxygen and they're doing tests to find out what's caused it." "She's really ill, and I'm very worried about her, I can't bear to think about losing her, it would be so bad, and I dread to think what it would do to my parents." Rebecca was crying again. Tim looked at her thoughtfully. "Ask Merva for her help," he said. Rebecca stopped crying momentarily and stared at Tim. "What do you mean?" she said, in a pleading manner. Tim stood directly in front of Rebecca and took both her hands in his. "This is from Vortan; he is saying that his mother, Merva was the greatest healer in all the land, she was the most renowned druid of her time, kings and great warriors from all lands travelled great distances to be treated by her and sometimes, simply seeking her council." "What's more, Merva has taken a great liking to you, and she wants you to try and continue her work, he says she wishes to help you and guide you, if you will agree." "What does all that mean?" asked Rebecca. "It means," Said Tim, "that if you agree, Merva will help you to become a spiritual healer, and if Merva's past reputation is anything to go by you would be a very powerful one." Tim paused then asked Rebecca, "So what do you think, do you fancy being a healer?" Rebecca paused thoughtfully for a moment, then answered. "I would like to be able to help my baby sister, she's in a bad state and I'm really worried about her, and if Merva can do anything to help her, I will be forever grateful to her, and I'll will do whatever she asks!" Tim nodded his approval. "Let's go to the hospital shall we and see if we can help?"

Rebecca, Tim and Hotpot arrived at the hospital and found the ward where baby Ashley was. Outside the ward Rebecca's parents sat. "What's happening?" said Rebecca to her mother. "The doctor's in with her at the moment, we'll see what he has to say when he comes out." Rebecca stepped over to the window of the ward so she could see what was happening inside. Rebecca's mum turned to Tim. "Hello Tim, what are you doing here? I though you didn't like hospitals." "I don't," said Tim, "but Rebecca is very worried about little Ashley, and she wanted to be close, so we brought her along, do you think she could go in and she her on her own for a few minutes?" Both Rebecca's parents looked at each other with a puzzled look. "Please?" said Tim, "just for a few minutes?" "OK." They both agreed. The doctor came out, but he looked very serious. He took Rebecca's mum and dad to one side and spoke to them quietly. Rebecca took the opportunity to go in and see little Ashley on her own. The baby looked fragile in the little oxygen tent. Rebecca paused, beside the baby, then put her hands together and closed her eyes. When she opened her eyes, she gasped as she saw Merva stood on the other side of the bed. She had prayed to Merva, but she was still shocked to see her. Merva smiled at Rebecca then nodded to her. Rebecca seemed to understand what she wanted her to do. She reached through the plastic cover and took hold of baby Ashley's hand, just then the space all around the baby seemed to go brighter and start to sparkle. The next thing Merva was stood next to Rebecca, she placed her hand on Rebecca's shoulder, and Rebecca let go of the baby's hand, she turned to Merva and they both embraced, at which point Merva disappeared. Rebecca's parents and the doctor came into the room, her mum took hold of her hand and spoke softly to her. "Sweetheart, Ashley is very ill, and the doctor says we must be strong because we can only wait and see how she does in the next twenty-four hours, it doesn't look very good for her." Rebecca looked at mother, smiled and said, "The baby is fine now!" They all looked strangely at Rebecca; the doctor quickly went to check on the baby. After checking her heart, pulse and breathing, he turned to Rebecca's parents, with an astonished look on his face. "What is it?" said the father. "What's wrong?" The doctor stared at them with a strange look on his face.

"She's fine!" he said, "everything is perfect, her breathing, her heart, everything is perfect, I don't understand, just a few minutes ago she was seriously ill, now everything is perfect, it's incredible!" he said. Rebecca smiled and said, "Its magic!" as she walked out of the ward to join Tim and hotpot. "How is she?" asked Tim. "She's fine." Said Rebecca, "thanks to Merva." "What do you mean?" said Hotpot. "Well," said Rebecca, "I asked Merva for her help, and she duly obliged, and the baby is fine now." She laughed as she said, "the doctor and my parents are a bit confused; they don't understand what's happened, I can't really tell them about Merva, can I?" They all had a little laugh. "Shall we go home?" said Rebecca, "I think Ashley is going be alright now, thanks to Merva, so I feel really happy and I'm so grateful to Merva, she's wonderful!" Tim thought for a moment, then spoke to Rebecca. "Remember you did promise Merva that you would continue her work if she helped you!" Rebecca was deep in thought. "What's all that going to amount to, do you think?" she said. "I don't know." Said Tim, "but I'm sure Merva will soon let us know!" "First thing I must do," said Rebecca, "is go to the grove tomorrow morning and offer my thanks." "Will you come with me, you two?" "It is school tomorrow you know!" said Tim. "Yes, I know," said Rebecca, "but we could go early before school, couldn't we?" Hotpot looked horrified, as he said, "I hate getting up that early!" The other two burst out laughing. "Don't be so lazy laughed Tim just be at my house for seven O'clock, we won't be long!" "OK," said Hotpot, but don't make a habit of getting me up that early, it's really the middle of the night for me." Tim and Rebecca both laughed, as they all went home.

Early Monday morning and the three friends met at Tim's and went straight to the grove, Hotpot was grumbling about being half asleep, Rebecca brought a bowl of fruit as an offering to the gods. When they arrived at the grove Rebecca quickly put on her white robe and placed the bowl of fruit on the altar and stepped back a little, while Tim and Hotpot stood on either side of her. She raised her hands to the sky and said, "thank you so much for helping to heal my little sister, I am so grateful, thank you, thank you, thank you." Just then, Merva appeared in front of them on the opposite side of the altar, she looked very regal in her long white robe. Her resemblance to Rebecca was quite uncanny, she was tall, and she had long jet-black hair, just like Rebecca. She was of course much older in appearance, but if you were to look at both of them from behind in their white robes, you wouldn't be able to tell them apart. She then walked around to stand directly in front of them, she smiled and put her hand gently on each of their heads as she stepped along the line, pausing in front of each of them. Then just as suddenly, she disappeared. "Wow," said Hotpot, "I feel really strange. "What do you mean?" said Rebecca. "I feel all warm and exhilarated, said Hotpot." "I feel as if I've been touched by an angel!" He said, holding his hands out, palms upwards. "I think you have!" said Tim, "I think we all have," said Rebecca. They were all extremely excited about meeting Merva and the feelings it left them with. Rebecca took off her white robe and put it away in her shoulder bag and they set off for school. Tim spoke as they walked to the bus stop. "I want to say something to both of you." "I want to thank you for being such good friends, I feel so happy that my life has changed so much and that you have both stood by me through all these strange experiences, without laughing at me, or calling me a nut case." Rebecca, who was taller than both of them, put her arm around Tim's shoulders, as she spoke. "These experiences have changed all our lives for the better and we have you to thank, what do you think hotpot?" she said. "Absolutely," said Hotpot, "I have never felt so good, I feel as if I could fly right now, and it's not so long ago we used to hide in the corner at school, now we hold our heads up high and enjoy ourselves." "And It's all thanks to you Tim, it's we who should be grateful to you," he said. They all linked arms as they walked very happily to the bus stop.

CHAPTER TWENTY-NINE

LITTLE FRANKY

They caught the bus and travelled the couple of miles downtown to school. They were all happy and were walking the short distance from the bus stop to school when Tim stopped by one of the younger pupils who was sat on a garden wall. It was little Franky Price; he was a first-year student and he had only been at St Joe's for a few weeks. He was a very sad sight, sat there on the wall with his head down, his school bag had been kicked away and was spilling papers and books out onto the pavement. Tim gestured to Rebecca and Hotpot to wait a moment. He went over to little Franky and put his hand on his shoulder. "What's the matter mate?" Tim asked. Franky shook his head but didn't lift it up. Tim put his hand under Franky's chin and lifted his head. They were all horrified to see the state of Franky's face. He had two black eyes, badly swollen lips, the bottom one was also split and had been bleeding. Rebecca at once went and sat down beside Franky and put her arm around his shoulders and gave him a cuddle. Tim looked at him again and asked, "Who did this to you?" Franky looked at Tim with tears running from his bruised and swollen eyes, then put his head down again, without speaking. Rebecca stroked his head affectionately and spoke to him. "It's alright, we're your friends you can tell us what happened." "I can't!" said Franky. "Was it someone from school?" asked Tim. Franky shook his head. Tim thought for a moment, then put his hand under Franky's chin and lifted his head again. "Was it your dad?" Tim said firmly, while staring into his eyes. Franky didn't speak, but Tim had his answer. "It's alright!" said Tim, "I've been there, and I know the feeling." This seemed to strike a note with Franky, he looked at Tim questioningly. As he asked. "You mean your dad?" Tim nodded, then asked, "What was it for this time?" "I tried to stop him from beating up my mother again, so he laid into me." "How is your mother?" asked Tim. "I don't know," said Franky, "I just had to get out before he killed me." Tim thought for a moment, "why doesn't your mother go to the police and report him?" Franky let out a sigh, "he is the police!" he said despairingly. "What?" said Tim. "My dad's a policeman, said Franky!" Tim let out a long sigh. Tim looked at Rebecca and Hotpot. "I think we're going to have the morning of school," He said, "is that OK with you?" Rebecca nodded and Hotpot smiled, "that's fine by me," he said, "I don't like school anyway, you don't have to ask me twice." "Come on," said Tim, as he put his arm around Franky's shoulders, "let's go and check on your mother. Franky was very hesitant. "My dad might be there," he said nervously. "Good." said Tim, "we'll see what he has to say for himself." "Are you serious?" said Franky, "He'll kill us." Tim gave a little laugh, "I don't think so," he said, with an air of confidence.

It was only a few hundred yards to Franky's house, a nice private house with a large garden in a tree lined avenue. Franky was incredibly nervous, he didn't want to go near the place, but he was worried about his mother, so he bit his lip and took a deep breath. "Are you sure about this?" He said to Tim. "It's alright," said Tim, "we're all in this together now, you're not on your own anymore."

Tim banged on the front door, very loud and aggressive, Franky shrank away and got himself behind Rebecca. The door opened, a rather large heavy man stood looking at them, he had a beer belly and his breath reeked of Alcohol. "What's going on?" he growled, staring at the four of them, but before he could say anymore, he found himself hurtling forward in an almighty somersault, landing flat on his back on the front drive. The impact knocking the wind out of him, he was barely conscious when Tim leaned over him, hitting him square in the face several times in rapid succession. Poor Franky jumped back in amazement, looking at his bully of a father spread out on the ground, a huge split above his left eye, poring with blood, a broken nose and a busted-up mouth all bleeding freely. Tim looked up at the others and told them to go and check on Franky's mother, while he sat on the step and watched over the sorry sight in front of him.

Franky stepped over his father on the ground, followed by Hotpot and Rebecca, they dashed into the living room where Franky's mother was lying on the couch. She was half asleep and opened her eyes as Franky went to her, she held out her hand to him. She was bruised all over her face and arms. Franky knelt next to her and put his arms around her and gave her a cuddle. "Where's is he?" she asked, with fear in her eyes. "It's alright!" said Franky, "some friends have come to help, and I don't think he's in any position to hurt anyone at the moment." He introduced Rebecca and Hotpot to his mother, but she was very confused. "What's happened? Where's your father?" she asked as she struggled to ease herself up from the couch. "Just relax," said Rebecca, he's not going to hurt you now."

Meanwhile outside, Tim sat on the step waiting for the bully to regain consciousness. Eventually he started to come round, first opening his eyes and looking round, then shaking his head, wondering what was happening. He put his hands up to his face and winced as he felt the pain and the blood. "What happened?" he said. Tim stared at him and replied. "You picked on the wrong one this time, that's what happened!" "Who are you?" asked the thug. "I'm a friend of Frankie's and I'm here to tell you that if you touch him or his mother again, I will come after you and I will make you pay!" "Do you understand that?" "I'm a police officer you know," the thug said. Tim reached over and took hold of the man's throat with his left hand and squeezed; clenched his right fist and stuck it into the man's face. "Being a police officer won't save you, and this is the only warning you're going to get, ignore it and you'll be sorry; also, if I was you I'd find somewhere else to live," said Tim, forcefully, your health is in danger hear. The thug struggled up from the ground and staggered to the car in the drive, he climbed into the car and sat there wondering what to do next. Tim gave him a very serious look then went into the house. He found Rebecca and the others in the living room. Franky introduced Tim to his mother, who was still looking very shook up. "How long has this been going on?" asked Tim. Franky's mother shook her head, she looked ashamed as she answered, "years now," she said, "I should have done something about it before now, but I was too frightened, it's gotten completely out of control." Then she looked around the room hesitantly. "Where is he?" she said nervously. "I think he's probably gone to the hospital to get his injuries seen to," said Tim. "What injuries?" she said in a confused voice.

"Oh," said Tim. "He met someone who wasn't afraid of him and was more than a match for his thuggery, but he's still alive." Franky's mother looked more confused. "Anyway," said Tim. "Never mind about him, let's see if we can do something about your injuries, and Franky's." He turned to Rebecca. "Can you help Franky's mum, and I will see to Franky." Rebecca nodded, and Tim took Franky into the kitchen, where he sat him down and placed his hands on Franky's head, he closed his eyes and mumbled a little prayer. Franky was staring at Tim, wondering what he was doing. Rebecca had been doing something similar with Franky's mother. "Come on," said Tim, "let's go and see how your mother's doing." They went back into the living room, where all three were sat on the couch. "Wow!" said Franky, as he realized all his mother's bruises had disappeared, "How did that happen," "What?" said Franky's mum, not realizing that all her injuries had been completely healed. Then she noticed that Franky's bruising had all gone. "Oh, my goodness, your face, it's all cleared up; how did that happen?" she said. "Go and have a look in the mirror," said Rebecca. Franky's mum got up from the couch and went over to the mirror on the opposite side of the room. As she looked into the mirror and saw that all the cuts and bruises had completely disappeared, she then looked down at her arms. "That's incredible!" she said, touching her face and arms with her fingers and shaking her head in disbelief. "How did you do that?" she said, looking at Rebecca. "Its magic," said Rebecca smiling; just sit down and I will make you a cup of tea." Franky sat with his mum on the couch, while Tim took hold of a foot stool and sat down in front of them. He looked at both of them. "You mustn't allow him to get away with this violence, it will just get worse and worse!" he said. "How can I stop him?" she said despairingly. "I can't stand up to him!" "I can!" said Tim.

"So, if you have any more trouble with him, just get a message to any of us and we will come and help you, and perhaps you should change the locks and keep him out of the house altogether." "Anyway, we will stay with you for today, so just relax and don't worry." "Thank you so much for your help," said Franky's mother, with tears running down her face. "How can we ever repay you?" "It's quite alright," said Tim." "We all need a little help sometimes, don't we?" Tim, Rebecca and Hotpot stayed with Franky and his mother until teatime without any further trouble, they left a couple of phone numbers for them to contact if needed and went home. They also agreed that they would call for Franky each morning for the rest of the week, just to make sure everything was all right.

They were happy that they had done some good for someone that really needed their help. On the way home they discussed the day's events. Hotpot said to Tim, "do you think you are becoming more and more violent?" Tim laughed, "It's not me, it's Vortan, I'm very quiet and timid, I wouldn't fight with anybody, you know that don't you." "Ha," scoffed Hotpot, "I don't know anything anymore, I can't tell where you leave off and Vortan takes over, I think you are changing more and more into Vortan!" Tim laughed, "I think you might be right about that; I feel as though I'm leaving the old Tim behind." "Well don't lose him altogether," said Hotpot, "I liked the old Tim, and I don't want to spend the rest of my life half killing people," aid Hotpot. "I agree with you," said Tim. "I don't either, but we don't just hurt people, do we?" He said, seriously. "We have helped people in other ways, haven't we?" "We certainly have, said Rebecca." "And that is something we could not have done just a short time ago, so don't you be knocking the changes we have all gone through," she directed her remark at Hotpot. "We have all benefited from Vortan's intervention," she said. "OK," said Hotpot, "stop shouting at me!" "I just don't want to see Tim turn into a raging killer!" he said. "Don't worry," said Tim, "I'm not going to disappear, and Vortan was not just a killer, he was the son of a great Druid, and he had much wisdom, he was also a very good healer, so I don't think we should be concerned." They all agreed.

When Tim arrived home his mother was waiting for him. You're late Tim, what have you been up to? I hope you haven't gotten into any trouble?" she said. Tim decided he should be open and honest with his mother about Franky and his mother, and their problems with the violent policeman farther. He explained what had happened and that they had missed school today because of it. He said he was sorry about missing school, but he thought it was more important to help Franky and his mother. Tim's mother was very understanding about the events as she and Tim had suffered the very same misery for years, at the hands of Duncan. She congratulated Tim for being so caring about others, but she warned him about getting involved with the police. Pointing out that Duncan's death had still not been resolved completely, and it would be better if he was not under any kind of suspicion or involved in any way. Tim agreed and promised to be careful but reassured his mother that at the time of Duncan's death he had been at her bedside in the hospital. "OK," she said, "I believe you but we both know what Vortan is capable of, don't we?" Tim nodded, and went up to his room, and lay on his bed.

CHAPTER THIRTY

VORTAN'S LIFE

Tim turned his thoughts to Vortan. "I would like to know some more about your life in Terravan, your life as a warrior." "OK, just relax." said Vortan, "I'll recall my memories of a time when three children from our tribe were stolen and carried off by Cunai tribesmen." Tim closed his eyes and allowed his mind to become immersed in Vortan's thoughts. He found himself looking at a commotion going on in the settlement. Women screaming, running around waving their arms shouting, grabbing hold of their children and bundling them into their huts. The disturbance had brought Merva from her grand hut in the middle of the compound, Tim recognized her right away from his own experiences with her, although he was now looking through Vortan's eyes. She appeared in her now familiar white robe, her beautiful jet-black hair flowing and reaching down to her waist. She looked all around the compound and enquired what was happening. One of the women rushed towards Merva and explained that three of the children had been abducted by Cunai warriors, there had been four, boys, but one had escaped. They had been playing hunting in the woods with wooden spears. They were about seven or eight years old and would have been considered a prise catch for the enemy tribesmen. The boy that escaped had dived under a bush and hid when he saw the tribesmen approach. Unfortunately, he stayed there a long time in fear, before appearing from under the bush and running back to the village to raise the alarm.

Merva looked straight at Vortan and gave him instructions. Vortan's warriors were already running from all around the settlement. From the huts, the surrounding fields and the woods where they had dashed to investigate the place where the boys had been taken from. Vortan instructed those that hadn't brought their weapons to go and get them quickly. When all the warriors were assembled there appeared to be about fifty or more of them all armed with spears, swords, axes and some with bows. Some of them were putting paint on their bodies, mostly blue, some were soaking their hair in white stuff, it looked like builders' lime to Tim, but apart from the paint and their weapons, they seemed to be wearing very little else. Although they were speaking this ancient language, Tim could actually understand what was going on, he was beginning to pick up on the language. Perhaps it was because he was seeing it through Vortan's mind, but however it was happening, Tim could understand what they were saying. Vortan's tribe had just a few horses and Vortan told two of the warriors to take horses and go ahead and track down the Cunai warriors with the stolen children. The rest of the party set off in a north easterly direction, tracking from the woods where the children were taken from.

They spent most of that day moving quickly through woods and crossing streams climbing hills, but very quietly, hardly a word spoken, using hand signals rather than speaking. Towards sundown one of the horsemen returned. He said they had caught up with the Cunai, who were preparing to bed down for the night. They were about an hour's walk ahead; the other horseman had stayed to keep watch on them. "Did you see the children?" Vortan asked the horseman. The horseman shook his head. "We didn't get so close, but I didn't see any children lord," he said.

Vortan looked up at the moon rising in the east, then turned to look at the remnants of the setting sun in the west, he was deep in thought, and he was deeply troubled. He sat on a bolder and stared at the setting sun in the west. After a few moments he called his most trusted warrior: Toplin, who was a seasoned warrior with many scars and many trophies, he was a large man with broad shoulders. He carried a large heavy spear in his right hand and a long bronze sword in a leather scabbard hanging from a wide belt. He was a fearsome looking man who never seemed to smile, even when everyone else was laughing. Vortan talked to him about his thoughts.

"I think we have been tricked, I think this party is a decoy, they're heading northeast." "The Cunai don't live northeast, they live northwards." I think the boys have been taken straight northwards." Vortan told Toplin to take twenty warriors and follow this party and deal with them. He also told Toplin to find out as much as he could from the Cunai warriors. Toplin selected his warriors and set off at a jogging pace in a north-easterly direction, following the horseman guide.

Meanwhile Vortan led the remaining thirty or so warriors westwards in an effort to intercept the Cunai party with the captured children. They rested for about two hours then set off at a fast-walking pace following the path of the moon to the west. After travelling through most of the night Vortan's party arrived at the area where they thought the other Cunai party with the children would be progressing northwards. Vortan instructed six warriors to search the area to see if they had passed or if there were any signs of them having been in the area, while the rest of the party settled down and took the opportunity to eat and rest. The warriors carried food in small pouches slung over their shoulders, mostly dried, cooked meat and fruit. When the scouting warriors returned one of them said he had found an encampment, but the party had gone. Vortan told his party to rest well because when they set off, they were going to be moving fast. The warriors seemed to have complete faith in Vortan, as they had travelled hard through the night, but were still prepared to continue even harder, after an hour's rest. There was no complaining or disagreement from them. They seemed to be dedicated to Vortan and the rescue of the children. The warrior who had found the encampment guided them to the place. Vortan asked his warriors to keep out while he inspected the site. He walked carefully around the site, touched the remains of the fire, and then searched the edge of the site for evidence of the Cunai's exit, northwards.

Vortan then sat down on a bolder, deep in thought, he closed his eyes and seemed to go into a trance momentarily. The warriors appeared to understand this and didn't move but watched Vortan intently waiting for his response. "We must hurry!" said Vortan as he opened his eyes. "The boys are not in a good state, and they are in real danger, we must hurry." This seemed to fire up the warriors as they set off northwards at a jogging pace. They picked up the trail of the Cunai party and stuck with it for the rest of the day. Tim figured out that it was Autumn or Winter time, as the day was short and there were few leaves on the trees, tracking was difficult because of the undergrowth and the intermittent rain, but travelling must have been just as difficult for the Cunai especially as they also had the children to slow them down. When dusk arrived Vortan gestured to the party to rest, but no fires, while he and three other warriors continued in order to find the Cunai, who were now very close. It was then that Tim became aware that some of Vortan's warriors were women, the three warriors that were chosen to go forward with him were all women. Tim hadn't noticed them before; they didn't look a lot different from the male warriors apart from the obvious. They were covered in war paint, mostly blue, but with some green, and the usual white starchy substance making their hair stand up as if they'd seen a ghost. They looked every bit as fearsome and dangerous as any of the other warriors, but there was a difference. They didn't carry spears, they all carried axes and knives, but their favourite weapon seemed to be bows. They all appeared to handle their bows with great care, they had pouches tied around their waists, packed with arrows. They were tall, silent and very serious. They were not there just to make up the numbers, they were very much respected by the other warriors. They had been chosen to go forward for a reason, they were especially good at stealth tactics, (sneaking up on people), silent killers.

It was dark now and the four left the rest behind and moved further north, quietly, pursuing the Cunai.

They hadn't travelled very long, when they saw fires in the distance. This inspired greater caution with the four, as they approached the Cunai encampment. The Cunai tribesmen were not so careful, they were chatting and laughing as they sat round eating and drinking. There appeared to be about twenty or more of them. This was more than Vortan expected, perhaps they had met up with others who had stayed here waiting for them. Vortan and his three women warriors crouched down low and crept closer to the encampment. They could see that the three captive boys were safe, but they were all tied together with hide ropes around their necks. They looked frightened and sad; they had obviously been beaten. They were bruised and dishevelled, they were a sorry sight. Vortan signalled his warriors to circle around the camp and position themselves closer to the children and wait. Then Vortan retraced his steps back to the rest of his warriors. "Let them sleep," said Vortan, referring to the Cunai. We will rest for a while and let them settle. It was a dark and gloomy night; the clouds were heavy and there was very little light from the moon. Vortan rousted his warriors and they set off northwards, they travelled the short distance to the Cunai encampment moving silently through the ferns and brush grass. They had been given their final orders and they moved silently like a family of cats surrounding the Cunai camp. The bowmen in front, the spearmen crouched close behind. Vortan circled the camp silently and joined up with the three women warriors who were so well hidden it was difficult to find them.

On Vortan's signal the three women warriors calmly fixed long arrows in their bows and simultaneously let fly at the Cunai warriors that were closest to the boys. This was the signal for all hell to be unleashed on the Cunai tribe. Vortan had drawn his axe and sword from his belt, axe in right hand, sword in left. Tim was completely stunned by the savagery he was witnessing. Vortan had killed three Cunai warriors before they had chance to move, striking them either on the head or just below on the neck depending on how they were lying, all in less than five seconds, then screaming like a wild animal slashing and hacking at everything that moved. The three women warriors had dropped their bows and drawn long bronze knives from their belts. Having killed the Cunai warriors closest to the boys, they moved in quickly and dragged the boys away from the fighting and cut the restraints from their necks. They collected their treasured bows and hurriedly picked the boys up and carried them away from the camp southwards. Meanwhile Vortan and his warriors had delivered such brutal and devastating vengeance on the Cunai tribesmen, Tim could hardly take it all in. The blood and the carnage were completely beyond Tim's comprehension. He realised that what he had seen of Vortan in the past was nothing to compare with what he had just witnessed. Vortan had killed at least five, probably six warriors in less than a minute. Tim couldn't imagine such savagery. Also, the whole event was completely one sided. At the end of the carnage every single Cunai warrior lay dead, and as if that wasn't enough, they were all decapitated and their heads taken as trophies.

Vortan's planning and organization had been so efficient that not one of his warriors, or the child captives had died. There had been a few wounds and injuries amongst his warriors, but this didn't compare with the carnage on the other side.

Having stripped the Cunai dead of their weapons and valuables, Vortan's party set off back southwards to their home. The captured boys had been revitalized with food and water, but most of all they were just relieved to be back with their own people. Perhaps the boys had become aware of the real danger that they were in, just as Vortan had in his previous day's vision. Vortan indicated that if the Cunai had seen them coming, the first thing they would have done, was kill the boys. Maybe this could account for his ruthless efficiency and outright brutality. The whole experience had sickened Tim. After a few hours travelling south they met up with the horsemen from the other party. Tim noticed that they had severed heads hanging from their saddles, tied by the hair. Vortan said they would rest here and wait for the rest of the party. After an hour or so Toplin and his warriors arrived. Tim could see that they also were carrying severed heads and extra weapons. Toplin nodded to Vortan, he was a man of few words, but he looked quite satisfied with his accomplishment. They were all incredibly pleased to see that Vortan and the other party had recovered the boys safely. As the whole party travelled back home Vortan suggested, it would be a long time before the Cunai would think about travelling south again.

When the party arrived back home, they were met by dozens of women and children as they approached the settlement. They all rushed to see if the boys had been rescued. The boy's families, especially their mothers were overjoyed to see them intact. When they crossed the wooden bridge over the deep stream and through the gateway into the compound, Merva was stood there waiting for them.

She was serious and solemn; she surveyed the returning war party with questioning eyes. She waited for Vortan to approach and report. Then she nodded her approval towards Vortan and the rest of the party and gently touched him on the head with her outstretched right hand. Then she walked amongst the warriors, touching them and thanking them for their efforts and bringing the boys back home safe. She finished by taking the boys by the hands into her grand hut and sitting them down on soft animal furs, she gave each of them a drink from a large jug, them spoke gently to them for a few minutes. She reassured them that they had done nothing wrong, and that they had been very brave, and she was really proud of them. She put her hands gently on each boy's head in turn and mumbled a short prayer. The boys then ran to their mothers, where they were spoiled with hugs and kisses. Within a few minutes the three boys were fast asleep in their huts, and everyone in the tribe was jubilant. A celebration and ritual were organized for that evening.

Tim was awoken by his mother Tina. "What is the matter with you? Tim, I've been calling you, your dinner is ready! You must have been in a deep sleep." Tim smiled. "OK, I'm coming down now." As Tim reflected on the events of his vision of Vortan's memory he realized that Vortan's life was much more violent than he had previously imagined. He knew it was a violent time, but couldn't actually get his head round the idea killing of people so readily and then cutting off their heads as a trophy, it was just too much to take in. When he thought how quick and efficient Vortan was at killing, he realized how it must have been difficult for him to restrain from killing people in modern times when he was faced with an adversary, and just hurting them instead.

He also began to understand how Vortan had been called 'The Slayer.' He was a fearful and devastating warrior. A killing machine. Tim thought, he was glad Vortan was on his side. He certainly wouldn't like to be opposed to someone like Vortan. He was just reflecting on these thoughts when he heard the voice in his head. "You don't have to think about that Tim! You are Vortan now!" It was Vortan, trying to reassure Tim that they were now one, and that he (Tim) is really a Celtic Warrior. Tim found this quite unnerving.

He had changed a lot since meeting up with Vortan, but to think about himself as the warrior that would kill people so readily simply just didn't fit with him. It was just too much to take in. "Never mind!" said Vortan, we will change with the times we're living in, if people leave us alone, we will leave them alone, that's fair, isn't it?" "I suppose so," said Tim. "Anyway, we must go down and have dinner, and pretend that I'm just a normal boy for now. "Good," said Vortan. "There is something I would like to ask you about the three boys that you rescued before we go down," said Tim. "What would you like to know?" said Vortan. "I'd like to know how the boys felt after their ordeal?" and if they suffered any long-term effects?" "Well," said Vortan, "my mother,(Merva) was very good at healing, as you know, she healed their troubled minds as well as their physical injuries, she would have given them a sleeping drug which caused them to sleep for most of the next day, when they eventually woke up their injuries had disappeared and they were in good spirits." "They also grew up to be fine warriors eventually." Tim found the whole experience very exhausting but a good insight into Vortan's difficult but exciting life. He thought that, to live in such a violent world and still become the absolute best warrior of your time, Vortan must have been an incredibly special person. 'Time for dinner.'

"What on earth is the matter with you Tim?" I've been calling you for ages, you must have been in a deep sleep," said his mum, (Tina). "Not really sleeping," said Tim, but Vortan was showing me some of his memories!" "Oh," said Tina, "and was it interesting," "It was intense," said Tim. "I'm beginning to understand why Vortan is so violent and aggressive, plus, how skilful and efficient he really was; is." Tina thought for a moment. "What do you think about your life since you found Vortan?" asked Tina. "My life has completely changed, and very much for the better," said Tim, "although, I'm only just beginning to understand what Vortan's life was really like, and how difficult it must be for him to restrain himself now, when we are presented with violent people." "Having seen the way, he dealt with his enemies in the past, and how efficient he is at killing, it frightens me just thinking about it." "In spite of this, meeting up with Vortan has been a very positive event in my life." "Also, I think that everyone who has come in contact with Vortan, has derived some benefit from his presence, except of course, for our enemies." "Well, that's true," said Tina thoughtfully. Tim had dinner and retired to his bedroom with his thoughts.

CHAPTER THIRTY-ONE

LITTLE FRANKY

Next morning Tim met up with Hotpot and Rebecca at the bus stop on the way to school. Then as agreed they went along to little Franky's to check on him and his mother, and to walk to school with Franky. Both Franky and his mother were OK but looked rather nervous. "Thank you all so much for your help, and also for coming for Franky, you're so kind," said Franky's mum. "Franky has only been at that school for a few months, and he hasn't enjoyed it one bit, I think perhaps there are a few bullies there, do you think you could keep a look out for him until he settles in?" she said. "Don't worry," said Tim, "Franky will be fine, we'll look after him, but what about you? Are you expecting the bully back today?" "I don't know," she said, "I'll just have to hope for the best." "That's not a good idea," said Tim. "My mother and I suffered the same kind of treatment for years, and there are people that can help." "My mother works in the library, and she can put you in touch with someone, she knows about your situation, her name is Tina and if you go and see her, she will help." "Please go and see her," said Tim.

The four walked the short distance to school, Tim reassured Franky that he would be OK. When they arrived at the school yard, Tim told Franky to walk on ahead so he could see if anyone was picking on him, but nobody bothered him, so they all went into class and got on with their lessons happily. Break time, Tim and Hotpot met up with Rebecca in the yard, they looked around for Franky but couldn't find him. They went over to some boys that were in Franky's class and asked if they knew where he was. The boys started laughing and giggling. Tim, Hotpot and Rebecca all recognized the signs and became incensed. Hotpot feeling angry took the initiative. He reached out and took hold of the nearest of the boys by his jumper and pulled him close. "Where's Franky? You little rat, tell me now? Demanded Hotpot, pushing his face very close to the boy's face. Tim and Rebecca were amazed at Hotpot's aggression, even if it was a younger boy, he had never shown any kind of violent behaviour before. The other boy quickly realized he was in trouble and stopped laughing. "Try the toilets," stuttered the boy. Hotpot looked at Tim and Rebecca, then let go of the boy, giving him an angry look. Hotpot, Tim and Rebecca then ran across the yard and into the toilet block.

They could hear a lot of laughing and shouting, they could see a group of boys gathered around one of the cubicles. Tim pushed his way through the group until he came to one boy holding another boy's head down the toilet. The boy doing the holding was a biggish boy with curly ginger hair and a red face. He looked round at Tim, but it was too late. Tim had hold of him by the hair and slammed him down onto the floor, dragging the other boy's head out of the toilet bowl and piling him on top of the ginger boy. It was then they could see that the victim was Franky. He was soaking wet and very distressed. Tim took hold of the ginger boy dragged him to his feet and rammed his head down the toilet bowl and flushed the cistern. He held the boy's head in the water for about ten seconds then dragged him out and held him on the floor by the throat. "Go anywhere near Franky again and you'll be going to hospital! Do you understand me?" growled Tim. The ginger boy couldn't speak but nodded his head in agreement. Tim turned to the other boys who had been enjoying watching Franky being bullied. "Give me your jumper," demanded Tim, as he focussed on the nearest of the boys!" "NOW!" He shouted. The boy, seeing the anger in Tim's face, quickly took of his school jumper and handed it over. Tim used the jumper to dry Franky's hair and face, then threw it back at its owner. The gang had tried to disperse but Rebecca and Hotpot had prevented them leaving the area. Tim spoke to the gang. "If I catch any of you bullying anyone in this school in future, you will be in serious trouble, do you understand me?" They all nodded hesitantly. "Now go," shouted Tim.

They all hurriedly made their way out of the toilets. Tim turned to the ginger boy who seemed to be the leader of the gang, he was still on the floor, feeling rather sorry for himself. "Get up, and get out, and be very careful," said Tim, "I'm going to be watching you." Franky seamed reassured after seeing the treatment the bullies received from Tim and the others. Tim told him that he must tell them, right away, if anybody tries bullying him again. Franky agreed, and they all went to class. "I hate bullies!"

Tim said to himself as they walked. After school Tim, hotpot and Rebecca waited for Franky in the school yard and walked with him the short distance to his home.

Arriving at Franky's, his mother met them at the door, she must have been watching at the window. "What's wrong?" Franky asked his mother. "Nothing, but I've had the locks changed and your key won't fit the new lock!" Said his mother. "I have a new key for you." "Come on in everyone, I need to thank you for your help yesterday." "I don't know where you got the courage from to tackle that monster, but I'm glad you did," she said. "That's OK, we've all been on the receiving end of bullies before now, so we know what it feels like," said Tim. "Come and sit down and tell me all about yourselves, I would especially like to know how you managed to heal both Franky's and my injuries, like you did?" Tim, Rebecca and Hotpot all looked at one another and smiled. They couldn't really tell the truth; Franky and his mum would just laugh at them. Tim thought for a moment, then replied. "Well, we met this old lady, and she taught us how to do it." "And did she teach you how to fight like that also?" asked Franky's mum mockingly. "Franky told me what you did to his dad, and that was not the actions of a thirteen-year-old boy, was it? Tim hesitated, then asked, "Did you go and see my mother like I suggested?" Franky's mum smiled. "Yes, I did, and you're changing the subject, aren't you?" "Was she any help?" asked Tim, persisting. "Yes, she was and I'm very grateful, but you still haven't explained how you managed to sort out my thug of a husband, who is six feet three and eighteen stone, an ex-rugby player and a trained police officer." "He was drunk!" said Tim, trying to explain away his newfound fighting prowess. "That doesn't account for what you did, does it?" said Franky's mum. "You wouldn't believe me if I told you." Declared Tim. "But there is something more important that we need to think about just now," said Tim, changing the subject again. "What's that?" asked Franky's mum. "I don't think you are entirely rid of your thug of a husband yet, and you need to think about how you are going to deal with him," said Tim. "I think you're probably right about that," said Franky's mum. "What do you suggest?" Tim thought for a moment. "I think his injuries will keep him occupied for a little while, but then I think he will come back looking for trouble, and when he finds the locks have been changed, he will probably become angry, "said Tim. "I agree," said Franky's mum. "So, what should I do to protect us from him, if he does come back," she said. "Firstly," said Tim, "you need to go to the court and get a restraining order, then I will come and stay with you for a while, in case he does come back." "You're very kind," said Franky's mum. "I don't know how to thank you, but I am very grateful." "You're welcome," said Tim. "In the meantime, if he comes back causing trouble, just give me a call and I will come straight away." "You're so kind, I don't know what we would have done if you hadn't come to our rescue, I can't really tell you how much difference it makes to have someone who understands what we've been going through." said Franky's mum. "The important thing is that you're no longer on your own," said Tim. "So, if he attacks you, he attacks all of us." "Thank you," said Franky's mum, with tears in her eyes. "Come on," said Tim "it's time to go. Rebecca and Hotpot went home with Tim.

The three friends kept a close eye on Franky at school and were pleased to see that the bullying appeared to cease, at least for the moment. At home Franky's mum had gone to the court and obtained an order excluding her husband from their house. She had also approached her solicitor about a divorce. Tim's mum agreed that he could stay at Franky's for a few nights but begged him to be very careful. Tim reassured his mum he would be careful and packed a bag and moved in to Franky's for a few days.

Franky's mum, (Rita) was pleased to see Tim with his bag. She had been incredibly nervous about her husband returning and causing trouble, especially since she had obtained a court order telling him to stay away from the house. Tim stayed in Franky's room at the front of the house, and all was quiet for the rest of the week. Apparently, Franky's father had been off work with the police, due to his injuries, but had been d. king a lot. His sergeant from work had called to see Rita and asked what had been going on. Particularly, why she had obtained a court order, keeping her husband away from the house. Rita reluctantly explained to the sergeant what had been happening for the last couple of years. With violence both to her and Franky. The sergeant was completely surprised to hear their story. He told Rita she should give them a call at once, if they have any further trouble. She agreed she would but was concerned as to whether he would be dealt with properly, because he was a police officer. Anyway, there was no trouble, for a further week.

Then, on Friday night at the end of the second week there was an. mighty bang at the front of the house. It was eleven thirty and the bang woke everyone in the house up with a start. Then there was a further bang. It was the front door, and it was Franky's father, and he was drunk. There was the sound of breaking glass. Tim was out of bed and dressed in seconds. Track suit and trainers. He was down the stairs and out of the back door. He had surveyed the house and garden in the time he had spent there. Through the side gate and on to the front drive. The brute stepped back a few paces to take a run at front door. He hadn't noticed Tim behind him. He growled as he prepared to charge the door once again. He was spitting mad, but before he knew what was happening Tim took hold of his shoulders from behind and slammed him down over an outstretched leg. The brute hit the floor with a frightening crunch. Tim leaned over him and punched him several times in the face, smashing his half-healed nose once again, and opening the cut over his eye, rendering him firmly unconscious. Franky's mum came to the damaged front door. She looked in amazement at the sight in front of her, then spoke to Tim. "I've called the police Tim, come in before they arrive." Tim stared down at the pathetic sight of the thug, fists still clenched, aggression in his eyes. Then he relaxed his hands as he looked up at Franky's mum. He nodded in agreement and stepped away from the pitiful heap on the front drive. Rita looked in disbelief as Tim stepped in past the shattered front door. "Go upstairs and get in bed before the police turn up," she said. Tim did as he was told and went straight upstairs, where he found Franky sat on his bed trembling with fright. "It's OK mate, he's not going to hurt you now," said Tim, as he put his arm round Franky's shoulders. He put Franky back into bed and got changed and went to bed himself.

The police arrived just as the brute was regaining consciousness. He struggled to his feet and staggered about the drive bewildered. Two police officers stepped out of their car and quickly surveyed the scene. They looked at the bully stumbling about, then at the damage to the front door. As they approached the bully, they could smell the stench of alcohol. They quickly came to their own conclusion and arrested him and bundled him into the car. One of the police officers came back to the house and asked Rita what had happened. "I'm not sure," said Rita, "we were all in bed when we heard this almighty banging at the front of the house." "I came down and found the door smashed to bits and him staggering about the drive just like you did." The police officer nodded and said he would call back later.

Rita went upstairs to check on the boys. They were sat up in bed talking. Tim was making light of the situation in an attempt to cheer up Franky, who was clearly extremely nervous and frightened. Rita forced a smile, realizing what Tim was doing. She looked at Tim. "Thank you once again, I don't know how you do it, but I'm so grateful to you, I think your mother must be very proud of you, you're such a caring person. Tim smiled, "my mother and I went through a very similar experience for years and I feel very strongly about bullies of any kind," he said. "Let's all see if we can get some sleep now shall we," said Rita.

In the event the bully was dealt with very severely, both by his employers the police, and by the court. The police suspended him from his job pending an enquiry. The court gave him a six-month suspended sentence and ordered him not to approach his wife or son, or their house. Perhaps the greatest penalty, was the shame and disgrace, the publicity brought upon him. He got what he deserved.

Tim went home in the morning, he explained to his mother everything that had happened. She impressed upon him the need to keep clear of the police. "I understand, but I didn't have a choice this time did I," said Tim.

"Tell me," Said Tina, "how did Vortan feel about sorting the policeman out?" "He wanted to kill him!" said Tim. "Really?" said Tina. "That's a bit extreme, isn't it?" "Perhaps it is, but in Vortan's world, somebody behaving like that would have been killed!" said Tim. "Vortan is struggling, trying to understand why we don't kill people like that!" "You should explain to him that we have more respect for life than to kill people so readily," said Tina. "He is trying!" said Tim.

Tina gave Tim a big hug and said how proud of him she was. She also said that the Bickerstaff's' had been on the phone asking why he hadn't been to see them for so long, and that they missed him very much. "I'll go and see them today." said Tim.

CHAPTER THIRTY-TWO

THE FARM

Rebecca and Hotpot came around to Tim's, after phoning to see if he was home. They all set off for the farm and Tim updated them on the happenings at Franky's as they walked.

"More violence!" said Hotpot, accusingly. "Shush!" said Rebecca, "If you were being bashed up, you'd be glad of someone intervening on your behalf, wouldn't you?" "I suppose so!" said Hotpot reluctantly. "Then stop complaining!" said Rebecca, defending Tim's actions.

When they arrived at the farm the Bickerstaff's' were so pleased to see them. "Where have you been for the last two weeks? We've missed you," said Mrs Bickerstaff. "Oh," said Tim, "I'm sorry; we have a little friend at school, and he was in trouble." "He was being beaten up by his drunken father, so we've been helping him, but I think he's OK now." After smothering them all with hugs and kisses, Mrs Bickerstaff took them inside and served up drinks and cake for everybody. "Come and tell us what you have all been up to," she said. They chatted for a while, Mr Bickerstaff explained that the sale of the water from the well was helping to pay off the debts to the bank and was actually starting to make the farm profitable, and it was all thanks to them for finding the well and suggesting that we could sell the water. "You have made such a difference to our lives," said Mr Bickerstaff." Tim thought for a moment. "I think it's more down to Vortan than any of us!" He spoke. Just then there was a knock at the door. Mr Bickerstaff answered the door, and to Tim's surprise it was his mother, Tina. "I didn't know you were coming," said Tim. "We asked her to come along because we had something to suggest, and we thought she should be here, I hope you don't mind," said Jack. The three friends all looked at one another quite confused. Tim, shaking his head enquired, "What are you talking about?"

"Well," said Mrs Bickerstaff (Mary), "Jack and I have decided that we would like to make you (Tim) our heir, which means leaving the farm and everything that goes with it to you. That is if you and your mother agree; what do you think?" Tim stood looking at them with his mouth wide open for a few seconds. "I don't know what to say," he said. "Well," said Mary, "We don't have any children of our own, and you have made such a difference to our lives, and anyway, we love you as if you are our own son." "The only other relative is Jack's sister Helen, and you have seen for yourself what she's worth, along with her thug of a husband, and anyway Helen has already had her share of their father's will." "When Jack inherited the farm Helen received all the money that was in the bank, which was a lot more than the Farm was worth." "As you have seen for yourselves Helen and her husband are not satisfied, they want everything, and we are determined that they're not going to get another penny." "So, we thought that if we leave everything to Tim the farm and everything that goes with it, would then be in safe hands." "Also, we would like to know that Vortan's grove and settlement would be preserved, along with the woods." "So really we're just returning Vortan's home back to his care." "So, what do you all think about this arrangement?" asked Mary. They all looked at each other in silence, they were all dumbstruck.

"Say something," said Jack. "I think it's wonderful," said Rebecca. "It means that nobody will ever spoil the grove or the old settlement which I think is very important for all of us, isn't it?" They all agreed, nodding their heads. "What do you think Tim?" asked Mary. "I think it's brilliant," answered Tim, "I'm just a bit overwhelmed, you're so kind, I don't really know what to say." Mary turned to Tim's mum, (Tina). "Is all this alright with you?" "Yes, of course, you're so kind, I just don't know what to say," said Tina. "You don't have to say anything," said Mary, "Let's all have a cup of tea." "Good idea!" said Jack. Tim turned to Hotpot. "What about you, you've been very quiet, what do you think about all this?" "It's brilliant, it means nobody will be able to spoil the woods, said Hotpot." Tim laughed. "I thought that would please you," he said. Tim thought for a moment. "What about Helen and her husband, they're not going to be very happy with this arrangement are they?" He spoke. "Don't worry about them," said Jack. "They have had all they're going to get from this farm." "Merva will be pleased." said Rebecca. They all agreed. "Come on, let's have a cup of tea and drink to Merva, and her memory," said Mary.

Tim Rebecca and Hotpot spent the next few days tidying up in the old settlement and then the grove. It was wintertime now and Hotpot was very keen to get everyone working in the woods, clearing the paths and blockages in the brook. It wasn't the nicest of work, but they all mucked in, along with Mr Bickerstaff and after a few days the whole place was looking quite nice and tidy. They all felt more attached to the place now, they were beginning to feel like they belonged there. It was like they were all becoming one big family, with Vortan and Merva in the background looking after them. Even though it was winter now the whole place seemed to be happy and bright. A new family of robins had moved in and built a nest in a bramble bush on the edge of the grove. There were a lot of swallows also about. It was changing so much from when Tim first came around with his metal detector. There were few birds or animals around the place then. It was very still and silent, quite stagnant in fact. Now there are rabbits, even a fox or a family of foxes. "What a change." Tim thought, as he looked around, feeling quite pleased with himself. He turned his thoughts inward to Vortan and asked, "what about the curse that your mother put on the place all those years ago, at the time of your last battle!" "Is that curse still in force!" Vortan paused for a moment, then replied. "Do you think all these birds and animals would be here if the curse was still on the place!"

"Merva cast out the curse after you awoke me from my long sleep and filled the place with joy and love and laughter." "Not just Merva," he said. "What do you mean?" said Tim, "not just Merva?" "I've told you before, said Vortan, the gods are smiling on you, they are pleased that you have come and brought new life and energy to the place!" "Whether you like it or not, you have been blessed by our ancient protectors!" "They are now your gods, and they are smiling on you and your friends and of course, your mother, so be happy." "Also remember, it is now your responsibility to look after the place." Tim nodded and agreed. "What are you nodding your head for?" said Rebecca, laughing at Tim. Who was stood in the middle of the grove, staring into space nodding his head. It looked funny. Tim snapped out of his trance-like state and looked at Rebecca and smiled. "Oh, I was just conversing with Vortan," said Tim. "And what did he have to say?" said Rebecca. "He was talking about his mother and the ancient gods," said Tim. Rebecca was intrigued. "Tell me about it," she said, "I really want to know about Merva and her life, she seems so interesting and unusual." Tim thought for moment.

CHAPTER THIRTY-THREE

TALKING TO MERVA

"Why don't you ask Merva yourself?" he said. "Don't be ridiculous," said Rebecca, "Merva isn't here, how can I ask her anything?" Tim smiled. "Are you sure she isn't here? Rebecca looked wide eyed at Tim. "What are you saying?" she asked. "Vortan says that if you close your eyes and ask Merva what you want to know, perhaps she will enlighten you," said Tim. "Are you joking with me?" asked Rebecca. "It won't hurt you to try, will it?" said Tim. "Anyway, you've seen her before, haven't you."

Rebecca thought for a moment then walked over to one of the logs that circled the altar in the grove and sat down. She closed her eyes and turned her thoughts to Merva.

Rebecca allowed her thoughts to drift to when the whole party was gathered around the old well and first Vortan, then Merva appeared and seemed to bless the whole party in turn. She was deep in thought reflecting on how warm and excited she felt on that occasion, and how honoured she was to be visited by such a powerful and influential druidic character from so long ago. Despite all her importance and power, Merva seemed to be so humble and simple.

Rebecca was sat there on the log with her eyes closed, smiling, when she felt the gentle touch of a hand on her right shoulder. She felt a strange chill spread over her. She opened her eyes and looked around. There was nobody there. Tim was over on the other side of the grove talking to Hotpot, who was up in the branches of an old oak tree, as usual. There was no one else in sight. She closed her eyes again and at once heard a voice in her head. "Rebecca," she heard the voice say. She opened her eyes and looked around again. There was no one there. She closed her eyes once more. "Don't be afraid," the voice said. "You wanted to talk to me, so I am here." "What would you like to talk about?" Rebecca realized it was Merva. "Is it really you?" asked Rebecca. "Relax my dear, you did want to talk to me, didn't you?" Rebecca was almost overcome with emotion. Her heart was racing, she was struggling to really believe that Merva was actually speaking to her. "Where are you?" asked Rebecca. "I'm here within you," replied Merva. "I have to communicate directly with your thoughts because you wouldn't understand my language!" "Oh, I see," said Rebecca, "but why can't I see you?" There was a pause for a few moments. "It is difficult for me to appear physically after all this time, though I can do so on occasions, I am more of a spiritual being now." "I have come to visit you, firstly because you and your friends have gone to so much trouble to restore my old settlement, and especially my sacred grove, and secondly because you asked for me." "So, what would you like to talk about?" Rebecca was just so excited she could hardly speak. She took a deep breath to calm herself down, then spoke hesitantly. "I would really like to know about you and your life here all those years ago and how you came to have such powers." There was a slight pause then Merva replied. "Well, my life here was mostly a very happy and fulfilling one, but it was a violent time, and all of our lives were affected by the violence." "In spite of that, for the most part life here was wonderful, we had everything we needed here, it was a beautiful place; if it hadn't been for the violence, it would have been a real paradise." "As far as healing powers are concerned, they are a gift from the gods." A gift that has been passed on to you, so you must learn to use it wisely. "I will, I promise," said Rebecca. Merva spoke again. "As far as the other things I was known for, it is a long quest." "What do you mean?" said Rebecca. "Well," said Merva, "the druids were known for their wisdom, their vocation was to guide their people along the right path." "In order to do that it was necessary to acquire much wisdom." "In order to acquire wisdom, it was necessary gain much knowledge." "To do that it meant absorbing a great deal of information." "That sounds very complicated," said Rebecca. "It simply means you have to study hard and take notice of wise people, Oh, and ask for help from the gods." said Merva. "How do I ask for help from the gods?" said Rebecca. "Simply do what you are doing now, find some quiet, close your eyes and speak to them, it's called praying," said Merva. "Can't I just speak to you?" asked Rebecca. "You can for now, but if you wish to make real progress you need to learn about the gods and what they stand for," said Merva. "OK," said Rebecca, "I promise I will try and learn as much as I can about the ancient gods." "Very good," said Merva, "but it is time for me to leave you now, I will come and meet with you again." Rebecca felt sad that Merva was leaving but she accepted it. "Thank you for coming to me," she said, "I feel so honoured and excited, I feel as though I have been touched by an angel." Then Merva was gone.

Rebecca blinked and opened her eyes to find Tim stood in front of her. "What's wrong?" asked Tim. "Nothing." Said Rebecca, "why do you ask?" "There are tears streaming down your face. Said Tim. Rebecca smiled. "I've never felt so wonderful in my life," she said as she stood up and gave Tim the biggest hug he had ever had. "What was that for?" asked Tim. "I just feel so good," said Rebecca. "I gather from your excitement you've been talking to Merva," said Tim. "I have," said Rebecca, "and it was just brilliant, I feel so excited, she's wonderful." "Tell Vortan thanks for his help in bringing Merva to visit me." "He hears you," said Tim, but I think Merva came to visit you because she wanted to, not because Vortan asked her." "Really," said Rebecca, "why do you think that?" "I think that she has chosen you to continue her work, or at least some of it," said Tim. "What do you mean?" said Rebecca. "Well, she has already showed you how to practice healing hasn't she?" said Tim. "You mean that was Merva?" Said Rebecca. "Of course, said Tim. "You don't think that I could do that for you, do you?" Rebecca smiled and danced around the grove like a happy fairy. "Come on," said Tim, "it's time to go home, if we can get Hotpot out of the trees for a few minutes."

Hotpot eventually came down from the trees and strolled across to the centre of the grove where Tim was standing. Rebecca was still dancing all around the grove. She danced over to hotpot and gave him a great big hug.

When she eventually let go, Hotpot stood with a bewildered look on his face. "What was that for?" he said. Rebecca just laughed and continued dancing round the grove. Hotpot looked at Tim. "She does that!" said Tim. After going across to the farmhouse and saying goodbye to Mr and Mrs Bickerstaff, the three friends set off for home. Rebecca in the middle linking arms with the two boys skipping along. They were all incredibly happy, but Rebecca was walking on air, "isn't life wonderful," she laughed. It had been an incredibly happy day all round.

The next few days the three friends spent as much time as they could after school, playing in the woods and around the grove and the old settlement. They had become remarkably close now, quite inseparable. Tim had developed a strange air of confidence but kept his quiet thoughtfulness he had always had. Hotpot was always quiet and shy but now seemed much happier than he had before Vortan appeared, he just loved being in the woods and climbing the trees, he treated them like his friends. Rebecca had completely changed from being withdrawn, not very happy and quite unhealthy, into a confident, happy, healthy and beautiful thirteen-year-old girl. Everything about her had changed from being teased and bullied about her glasses and round shoulders. She had gotten rid of her glasses pulled back her shoulders and seemed to grow several inches, her black hair shined like a mirror and everyone in the school yard wanted to be her friend, especially the boys.

CHAPTER THIRTY-FOUR

THE CHIEF INSPECTOR

One day Tim arrived home after spending the day with Rebecca and Hotpot down the farm. As he opened the back gate, he heard Vortan saying, "We've got problems." "What problems?" asked Tim. "I'm not sure, but there's someone waiting in the house." Tim took a deep breath and opened the back door and stepped inside. "Timothy," his mother called from the living room. "Coming." Replied Tim, feeling quite apprehensive, as he put his shoulder bag on a chair and went through to the living room. As he entered, he noticed a man sat opposite his mother, Tina. A large man, dark wavy hair, piecing dark eyes, he had eyebrows like dead caterpillars, a broad face and broad shoulders. He was wearing a dark blue suit and holding a hat, a trilby, or something like a trilby, his shoes were black and very shiny. "This is Detective Chief Inspector Battley Bonus," said Tim's mum. "He wants to talk to you about something."

Tim looked at the large man, then looked at his mother, he was apprehensive, but he was struggling to avoid bursting out laughing at the man's name. Battley Bonus. "I bet he was a good fighter at school," Tim thought to himself, "he'd need to be with a name like that." "What's up now?" said Tim. "It's alright," said the man, "I just want to talk to you about Duncan, your stepfather and his mysterious death." "How can I help, I was at the hospital with mother when he died, said Tim. "Please don't be upset," said the large policeman, putting his hat down on the arm of the settee where he was sitting, "I know you was at the hospital; I'm not accusing you of anything." "I also know that he had been very violent to both you and your mother over the years and off the record I think he got what he deserved, I have no time for thugs like him, and I can tell you I've seen a few of them in my time in the police." "It's just that we have received the autopsy report, and it seems that Duncan had some injuries that he had received shortly before his death, and I was wondering if you know how and when he acquired these injuries?"

Tim looked at his mother, she put her head down, not wanting to give anything away. "Duncan was always brawling, especially when he'd been drinking!" replied Tim, staring straight at the policeman. "Hmm," muttered the policeman thoughtfully. "Tell me Timothy, what do you think about the account of Duncan's death, given by his so-called friends?" Tim shook his head, "I don't know what they said, but in any case, I wouldn't take any notice of that gang anyway, they're just a bunch of drunkards!" "Most of them don't even know their own names by the time they fall out of the pub," said Tim, scornfully. "They were no better than Duncan really, they were all as bad as one another; drunken pigs," he said, not trying to hold back his feelings. The policeman raised his bushy black eyebrows at Tim's outspoken reply. "Well," said the Chief Inspector, "his friends said they were confronted by a strange looking man outside the pub, they said he was wearing blue paint with white stuff in his hair, and he was otherwise nude, and he was really wild." "Then, they said they all ran off because the weirdo attacked them and when they looked back, Duncan was on the floor and the weirdo was gone." "Then, when they went back to check on Duncan, he was kaput."

Tim heard Vortan's voice in his head, "be careful what you say," said Vortan. Tim smiled and nodded. The policeman looked at Tim's nodding and smiling. "Do you think that's funny?" he said. "Well, don't you?" asked Tim, smiling again and scoffing. "A nude man covered in Blue and white paint, attacking a gang of drunks, 'come on,' do you believe all that rubbish?" The policeman stroked his chin and nodded and smiled. "Now you're doing it," said Tim. "You must think it's funny as well." This brought a bigger smile to the face of the policeman. He'd tried to catch Tim out but had been caught out himself. "So, you don't believe their story then?" said the policeman, staring at Tim. "Give me a break, who would believe that stupid load of rubbish?" said Tim laughing out loud. "OK," said the policeman, "tell me, how are you getting on at school?" changing the subject. "Fine," said Tim. Getting another message from Vortan telling him to keep his answers short and not to get into too much conversation with the man.

"I believe you had some problems with some other boys some time ago," said the policeman. Tim thought for a moment. "Who doesn't have problems with bullies at school," he replied. "Well," said policeman, it's not every thirteen-year-old that can put four sixteen-year-olds in hospital, is it?" Tim shrugged his shoulders and replied, "What do you suggest I should have done? Perhaps let them beat both me and my mate up?" Tim went on. "All we were doing, was defending ourselves, is that wrong?" said Tim sternly.

Battley Bonus looked thoughtfully at Tim, scratching his chin. "I'm not suggesting that it was wrong! I'm just wondering where you learned to fight like that. Do you practice karate or boxing or something?" "No," snapped Tim, "I was just tired of being bullied and I thought it was time someone stood up to that thug and his gang, whatever the cost." "Anyway, I wasn't on my own, my mate, Hotpot was with me." "Hotpot!" laughed the policeman, "who's Hotpot?" "Sam," said Tim. "That's a ridicules name," said the policeman. "Ha," said Tim, "Look who's talking. "Timothy," said Tina, "Don't be cheeky," "Sorry," said Tim, "I couldn't resist." "It's quite alright," said the policeman, "I'm well used to people laughing at my name, but you know, I didn't pick it, I've had to live with it all my life and it hasn't been easy I can tell you, especially when I was at school." "I can believe that," said Tim.

"Anyway," said the chief inspector, "I must explain that I'm not an ordinary policeman, I am a specialist, and my speciality is serious crime with unusual phenomena." "Oh really," said Tina, "So what are you doing here." "Well," said the policeman, "you have to admit that Duncan's death is rather unusual, isn't it." He then turned to look at Tim with a strange inquisitive expression on his face. "Don't keep looking at me, I was at the hospital with mother, all night, I was there when the police came to tell us about it, so what do you expect me to tell you?" "OK," said the policeman, nodding his head in a knowing gesture. "I'll leave you in peace, for now, I will be back to speak to you again, and if there is anything you would like to speak to me about, you'll find me on this number." He handed Tina a card. As he was leaving, he gave Tim a strange look, as if he knew something. When he'd left Tina turned to Tim. "I think he knows something; you're going to have to be careful with him you know." "Yes, I agree," said Tim. "There is something about that man." "What do you mean?" said Tina. "He's psychic!" said Tim. "How do you know?" said Tina. "Vortan knows," said Tim. "Really," said Tina, "that's strange, how does he know that?" "He can read thoughts," said Tim. "The policeman is thinking that there is something strange about me, and that I am somehow connected with Duncan's death, but he doesn't know exactly how." "We'll just have to be extra careful," said Tina. "OK," said Tim.

CHAPTER THIRTY-FIVE

BIG TROUBLE

Saturday morning, Tim had done some shopping for his mother while she was at work. Rebecca and Hotpot came round, and they all set off for the farm. As they were walking down the private, cobbled lane leading to the farmhouse Tim stopped in his tracks. They were now in sight of the house, about fifty yards away. "What is it?" asked Rebecca with confused look. "Trouble," said Tim. "What kind of trouble?" asked Rebecca. "I'm not sure," said Tim, "but it's serious, I think you two should stay here and hide in the woods and watch." "I will go to the house and investigate." "If I'm not out in five minutes don't approach; go and get some help." "What kind of help?" asked Rebecca. "Have you got your phone with you?" asked Tim. "Yes," replied Rebecca. "Well phone the police and tell them anything you can think of to get them here, said Tim. He then continued down the lane and across the yard, his feeling of trouble increased, he paused and turned his thoughts inward to Vortan and asked if he could see what the trouble was. "It's Mr Bickerstaff's brother-in-law, big Harold, he's here and he's always trouble." Tim noticed that there were two unfamiliar cars by the house, he turned and nodded towards the edge of the woods where Rebecca and Hotpot were hiding. Instead of knocking on the door he sneaked along the flower bed and crouched down to steal a look through the living room window. He could see Jack and Mary sitting on the couch, they were arguing with big Harold, who was stood in front of them. Harold started pacing and as he turned to face them again Tim saw that he was holding a gun in his right hand. Tim pulled back in horror, sank to the floor with his back to the wall, just under the window. "What shall we do?" he asked Vortan. "I hesitate to say it, but I think they're waiting for you, and they know you're here." "Really," said Tim, "So what shall we do?" "Let's go in," said Vortan, "but be careful, there's someone else in there somewhere." Tim crept back along the flower bed to the front door, which was slightly open, he pushed it open further and stepped inside.

He blinked several times then opened his eyes wide. His head hurt, he looked all around, where was he. He didn't know this place. Then he realised he was bound hand and foot, lying on a bed there was a light on, a bare bulb hanging in the middle of a strange room. Where am I? what's happened? he thought. It took him a few minutes to focus his mind, even to remember his own name, and his last conscious memory. It was then he remembered stepping through the door at the farm and everything going black. That's why his head hurts, he thought, he must have been whacked on the head by someone waiting behind the door. Then he remembered seeing big Harold with a gun threatening Jack and Mary. "Vortan," he called out loud.

"Shush," came the voice in his head, "don't call out, I'm here with you." "Where am I? What's happening?" Said Tim. "Don't worry," said Vortan, "I will look after you, but you must do as I say because you are in serious danger." "These people are serious criminals, and we must deal with them accordingly." "What do you mean by that?" said Tim. "I mean that you have to let me deal with these people my way," said Vortan. "Does that mean what I think it means?" said Tim. "Understand this," said Vortan, "Your life is in danger, these people only have one principle and that is to get what they want whatever it takes, usually by stealing, or causing misery to others." "We mustn't underestimate them, or the measures they will go to, "said Vortan. "Now listen to me carefully, I'm going to leave you for a short time, I promise I will be back very soon, in the meantime just do as they say and don't cause any trouble." Then Vortan was gone.

Tim was on his own for the first time in what seemed like half a lifetime, even though it was only a matter of weeks since he had met up with Vortan. He had become comfortable with Vortan's presence, which was no easy task, now he felt uncomfortable without him there. He also knew that Vortan understood people, especially with his ability to read their thoughts. Tim also knew that Vortan was good at what he did best. Like it or not, he was a ruthless and very efficient warrior and Tim was prepared to give way to Vortan's judgement about this situation.

Tim looked around the room. The room which had become his prison. It was a lot to take in for a thirteen-year-old, he tried to figure out what had led to this situation. Thinking that big Harold was probably the driving force, it was something to do with the farm and money. Perhaps he had found out that the Bickerstaff's' had made a will leaving the farm to Tim. That wouldn't please him very much, Tim thought. Especially now that Merva's well water business was bringing in quite a lot of money. Tim wondered where this place was, he could hear the noise of traffic, the room seemed to be like a cellar, partially below ground level. There was a small window with bars on the outside, but it was dirty, and he couldn't see anything through it. The bed he was lying on smelled of urine. There was other furniture in the room, but it wasn't very nice, it was quite tatty, a chest of drawers, a small wardrobe, a table and two dining chairs, an easy chair, a TV set in the corner even, but everything looked old and cheap. Tim wasn't used to luxury, but his upbringing was respectable, and his house was always clean and tidy. This place was grimy, it would be bad enough without the bindings on his wrists and ankles.

Back at the farm Rebecca and Hotpot had been hiding in the grove watching. They couldn't see very well. All they saw was Tim sneaking around the farmhouse and looking through the windows, then going into the front door, then a few minutes later, two men coming out carrying something like a sack and putting it into the boot of one of the cars and drive off.

CHAPTER THIRTY-SIX

REBECCA AND HOTPOT

"What shall we do?" said Hotpot. "We'll do what Tim told us to do," said Rebecca. "We'll give it five minutes and then phone the police for help." "What will you say?" said Hotpot. "I don't know but, I'll think of something," she said. "Why don't you ask Merva what to do?" said hotpot. "That's not a bad idea," said Rebecca, "But I don't know if I can get through to her." "I will try though." With that in mind Rebecca stepped over to the stone altar and placed her hands on it, she closed her eyes and pleaded with Merva to come and help. She tried visualising Merva's image and how wonderful she felt the last time she appeared, but nothing happened. Discouraged she opened her eyes and looked around, there was nothing. She stepped a few yards over to one of the logs and sat down and put her head in her hands and rested it on her knees. "What is it my dear?" the voice said, at the same time Rebecca felt a hand on her shoulder. Startled she lifted her head and looked round. There was nothing there.

"Rebecca," the voice said again, "What is it? You called me." Rebecca stood up abruptly and looked all around, she couldn't see anything. "Merva," she muttered hesitantly. "I'm here within you." Rebecca felt a wave of emotion surge through her, one she had felt once before. "Please, I need, or we need your help, we think Tim is in trouble and we don't know what to do." There was a pause. Then Merva spoke to Rebecca. "Vortan will look after Tim, but you need to help Mr and Mrs Bickerstaff."

Hotpot had run over to his favourite oak tree on the edge of the grove and quickly climbed about fifteen feet up his tree and positioned himself behind the trunk on one of the lower heavy branches. He was switching his gaze from the farmhouse to Rebecca and back to the house. He looked at Rebecca apparently talking to herself and nodding her head. He quickly shinned down the tree and ran across to Rebecca. "What's happening?" he asked eagerly. "Merva says that Vortan will look after Tim, but we need to help Jack and Mary." Hotpot paused deep in thought, then crouched down low and hurried across to the farmhouse.

He positioned himself under the living room window and hesitantly peeked in. His jaw dropped as he took in the scene in the room. He pulled back in horror and crouched down under the window trying to make sense of the situation. He thought what Tim had said about waiting for a few minutes and then going for help. He also thought about what Merva had said, to help the Bickerstaff's'. He sat under the window wracking his brains. "What would Tim do," he thought. He looked over at Rebecca and gestured for her to get down. Rebecca quickly retreated to the woods and hid, watching Hotpot from behind a holly bush. Meanwhile Hotpot searched around the flower bed where he was crouching until he found a nice medium sized duck stone. He carefully dusted off the soil and stepped back. He thought that the first thing to do was to distract big Harold and get the Bickerstaff's' out of there.

He drew back and let fly with the duck stone right through the living room window. At the same time, he took off running like a rabbit back to the woods where Rebecca was waiting aghast at what he had just done. "Phone the Police!" he shouted as he joined Rebecca behind the holly bush. At the farmhouse there was an almighty crash as the stone came through the living room window. Big Harold panicked not knowing what was happening, he turned to Jack and Mary and shouted, "Your little friend is gunna die if you don't sign this place over to 'me and Helen,' you've got one hour." He then ran out of the house, jumped into his car and took off screaming the wheels and kicking up loads of dust and mud as he sped down the private farm road, the car rattling and banging on the uneven cobbles.

Rebecca phoned the police and was shouting trying to explain what was happening. Jack and Mary came running out of the house, looking around to see what had happened with the window.

Hotpot and Rebecca seeing that Big Harold had gone, came out from their hiding place and ran across to Jack and Mary. "What's happening?" Shouted Rebecca. "They've kidnapped Tim!" cried Mary, terribly upset as she slumped down onto the front wheel of Jack's tractor with her head in her hands. Jack tried to comfort her, but she was inconsolable. "Don't worry about Tim!" said Rebecca, aiming her remark at Mary. Mary lifted her tearful head from her hands and looked at Rebecca quizzically. "What do you mean?" she said. "I have spoken to Merva," said

Rebecca, "And she said Vortan will look after Tim." Mary seemed to be warmed by this news but was horrified when she found out that Rebecca had phoned the police. "Harold will kill him," she cried. "I don't think so," said Rebecca, "not with Vortan there."

CHAPTER THIRTY-SEVEN

VORTAN'S JUSTICE

Tim heard voices in the distance, in another room. He couldn't make out what they were saying but they were getting louder. Then an almighty scream and a crash and more shouting. Then it went quiet. Tim was very nervous; he was feeling very much alone and frightened. He had; since meeting Vortan become more courageous and felt stronger and much more positive, but now with Vortan gone he was feeling how he used to feel when he was being bullied at school and battered from pillar to post by his horrible stepfather.

"Where are you Vortan?" he felt himself calling out. "I'm right here," a voice came back. It was Vortan, and Tim let out a huge sigh of relief. "Where have been and what's going on?" he said. "Don't worry," said Vortan, everything is going to be alright, you just have to be patient." "What do you mean, I have to be patient, why don't you get these bindings off my hands and feet, they're really beginning to hurt," said Tim feeling increasingly confused. "Just hang on a little longer," said Vortan, "I'm staying with you, and we'll be out of here soon."

"Well just tell me what's going on then," said Tim painfully. There was a short silence, then Vortan spoke. "Fat Harold." Tim interrupted, "You mean Big Harold." "Yes, Big Harold, and his wife Helen found out that the farm was making money from the sale of the spring water, and they wanted their share. Then they found out that Jack and Mary were going to leave the farm to you." "That just sent them spinning out of control, they are just greedy people who can't stand to see Jack and Mary getting ahead." "So, what am I doing here, and come to think of it where am I?" said Tim. "This place is the back room of Big Harold's snooker club in the city, and he has threatened to kill you if they don't sign the farm over to them!" said Vortan seriously." Tim was so shocked to hear this he couldn't think straight. He eventually collected his thoughts. "Well why don't you get me out of here?" he said, more and more confused by now. "Soon," said Vortan. "But first I have to do something, I have to leave you again just for a few moments." "Don't leave me like this," said Tim nervously, "especially if they're going to kill me." "Don't worry," said Vortan. "I'm just going next door to wait for fat Harold, he's on his way and nobody is going to harm you, I promise." "It's Big Harold," said Tim but he was talking to himself.

Next door Vortan waited; wild Warrior mode, blue war paint, white hair stood on end, a fearsome sight. Outside a car screamed to a noisy halt. Big Harold jumped out, slammed the car door, spit on the pavement and kicked open the door and burst in. Coming inside from the bright daylight into the dimly lit room it was difficult to focus at first.

"Kill him!" shouted Harold as he saw his two henchmen stood at the far end of the number three snooker table. "Kill him," he shouted again, as he ran towards the two men, but then he recoiled in horror as he realised it wasn't the two men. It was two severed heads stuck on snooker cues rammed through the end pockets of the snooker table. He pulled back in shock as he looked down and saw the bodies in great pools of blood at his feet. Before he could collect his thoughts, Vortan had followed him from behind the door and whacked him on the back of the head with a piece of wood. Harold crashed to the floor in amongst the blood and the bodies unconscious. Vortan picked up the sword that had been used to decapitate the two thugs and placed it in Harold's hand. It was a Japanese sword from the collection of a dozen or more various kinds, decorating the wall behind the bar of the club.

Vortan returned to Tim in the back room of the club. "You're back you staying this time?" said Tim as Vortan joined him once more. "I'm staying with you, relax now," said Vortan. "The police are on the way, and we want them to find you tied up like you are, so just be patient for a little longer." "Why?" said Tim. "You'll see," said Vortan.

CHAPTER THIRTY-EIGHT

CHIEF INSPECTOR BATLEY BONUS

Police sirens sounded as several patrol cars entered the street and proceeded to cordon off the area. Who should be first on the scene. None other than Detective Chief Inspector Batley Bonus, he jumped out of the car and reached inside his jacket pocket and pulled out a handgun, he quickly checked it over and approached the door of the snooker club. The door was partially open, and he could look in, but he couldn't see very much as it was quite dark, although there were some low lighting.

He entered very cautiously as he had been informed that Big Harold had been carrying a gun and threatening the Bickerstaff's' with it. He also knew of Big Harold and his dodgy dealings. Although Tim had laughed at the policeman with his funny name, chief inspector Bonus was no fool. He was a very much respected detective with a reputation for being a real hard man. He levelled his gun at the sight of the two figures at the far end of the snooker table, then staring harder at the sight as his eyes began to adjust to the differing light he slowly approached, looking all around as he moved forward cautiously. Behind him came several armed officers who quickly moved all around the inner walls of the club searching every corner, pointing their guns as they went. "Oh my god," he called out as he stepped closer to the horrific sight. Then looking down at the gruesome sight on the floor he focussed on Harold who was just beginning to move and regain consciousness. The policeman reached down and removed the sword from Harold's hand and passed it to one of the other policemen who carefully placed it in a plastic bag. He gestured to another officer to put handcuffs on Harold. Meanwhile an officer opened the door to the passage leading to the back room. Inspector Bonus put his hand up to the officer telling him to wait, then stepped over to the passageway.

He carefully crept along the corridor to the door at the other end. Opening the door, he saw Tim on the bed. "In here," he shouted and dashed in to check on Tim. "What's happening," called Tim, staring fiercely at chief inspector Bonus. "It's alright now," said the large policeman as he took a pen knife out of his pocket and proceeded to cut the binding off Tim's wrists and ankles. "How are you feeling Tim?" said the policeman. "Confused!" said Tim. "What's happening?"

Chief inspector Bonus quickly looked around the small smelly room scrutinising every corner and checking if there was another door. He didn't want Tim to witness the horrific scene in the other room. "Are you hurt Tim?" asked the policeman. "My head hurts, but I think I'm alright otherwise," said Tim. Having taken off the bindings from Tim, the large policeman reached down and gently picked Tim up in his powerful arms. "Close your eyes, Tim," said the policeman, as he carried him along the dark passageway and into the main snooker room. "Why?" asked Tim. "Just do it," said the policeman. Tim closed his eyes but couldn't resist taking a peek as he was carried through, past the large tables. He was quite shocked when he saw the two severed heads stuck on snooker cues, but he pretended he hadn't seen anything. He had of course seen similar sights before, in his visions of Vortan's life and the aftermath of battles, so he wasn't as shocked as perhaps he should have been at such a sight. In the event he thought it better if he pretended he hadn't seen it at all.

CHAPTER THIRTY-NINE

IN THE HOSPITAL

Outside the large policeman gently put Tim into his police car and told his driver to take Tim to the hospital. "I'll be along shortly Tim, your mother is already on the way so just relax and let the doctors check you over, this officer will stay with you, I need to look around here for a few minutes."

In the hospital Tim was put in a private room and was being checked over by several doctors and nurses, then his mother burst into the room dashed over to Tim and gave him a big hug. "Oh, my baby what have they done to you?" she cried, tears running down her cheeks. "Mother! I'm alright stop panicking," laughed Tim. The doctors assured Tina that Tim was OK, and he would be allowed to go home when they had finished doing test, just to be sure. Then without warning the room door burst open and in rushed Hotpot and Rebecca. The policeman who was guarding Tim followed them in to check it was all right. Tim nodded and the policeman retreated to the corridor.

Rebecca dashed over to Tim and threw her arms around his neck and nearly squeezed him to death. Tina raised her eyebrows and looked at Hotpot. Hotpot just turned the palms of his hands upwards, shrugged his shoulders and said, "she does that!" "You're choking me!" said Tim, pulling Rebecca's arms from around his neck. She sat down on the edge of the bed and straightened up. "You idiot," she said, scolding Tim. "What did you think you were doing, going in there like that?" Tim paused for a moment, deep in thought. "I was worried about Jack and Mary!" he said, apologetically. Realizing that he'd been a bit reckless. Tim then turned to Hotpot. "Thanks for helping mate, I'm proud of you and Rebecca for watching my back."

"Do you know what really happened, or are you still confused?" Asked Tina. "I think so," said Tim. "Jack's sister Helen and her thug of a husband, big Harold decided that the farm was eventually making money because of the sale of the spring water, and they wanted to have their share. "Then, when they found out that the farm was being left to me, they completely flipped and threatened Jack and Mary and said they would kill me if jack didn't sign the farm over to them immediately." They must have been watching us arrive and had their henchmen standing behind the door when I played into their hands." "They must have clobbered me as I stepped through the door." "All I remember is waking up in some stinking room with my hands and feet tied up." Tina gave Tim another hug. "You must have been terrified," she said. "Not really!" said Tim. "Vortan was with me, and he assured me he would protect me, and he did."

Then a knock on the door of the private room and in walked the large figure of detective chief inspector

Batley Bonus. "How are you now Tim?" he growled in his deep voice. Rebecca and Hotpot stared at him with their mouths open. "I'm fine," said Tim. "Thank you for rescuing me, it was pretty horrible in that place, wasn't it?" "It certainly was," said the chief inspector, "but I want to ask you if you knew what was going on in the other room of the Snooker club." Tim thought for a moment. "I heard a commotion and some shouting and then it went quiet, soon after that you came, that's all I can tell you." "I was just glad to see you, my head was hurting, and I wasn't very comfortable with my hands and feet tied like that." The policeman nodded his head then leaned over and put his hand on Tim's shoulder. "You've been very brave and we're all proud of you!" "I would like to come and speak to you again when you've had chance to recover, but for now I think you should just rest and don't worry about anything, I'll leave this policeman hear until you go home!" "Thanks for everything," said Tina. "You acted very promptly when Rebecca phoned." "We've been watching Harold for some time," said the policeman. "He's been involved in a lot of bad stuff, but he won't be bothering you anymore where he's going." "He's going to be there for a long time, so don't worry about him." He said as he left the room.

Tina came and sat on the bed and held Tim's hand. "What did he mean about what was going on in the other room?" she asked Tim. Tim sighed, "I don't think you really want to know about that," said Tim. "Why?" asked Tina. "It was really gruesome!" said Tim. "Well, we're going to find out anyway, eventually, so you might as well tell us now," said Tina. "OK," said Tim, "but don't blame me when you throw up!" "Hear goes then; when the two thugs clobbered me, they bundled me into the boot of their car and took me to Big Harold's snooker club in the city." "They put me in the stinking back room, still tied up." "I don't really know what happened next, but when inspector Bonus was carrying me out I took a peek and saw the two thugs had been decapitated and their heads were stuck on sticks at the end of a snooker table by the entrance to the passageway leading to the back room where I was being kept." Tim looked around at his mother and his two friends. They were all staring at him with their mouths open. "Are you serious?" said Tina, "or are you trying to scare us?" "I told you it was Gruesome," said Tim. "Who did that?" said Tina. "Well, I didn't see any of it, so I don't really know, but I could have a good guess," said Tim. "Oh no," said Tina, you don't think it was Vortan, do you?"

Tim was deep in thought for a moment, then he spoke. "The way that those heads were positioned at the entrance to the passageway and the way that they were stuck on poles like that; it's the way that the Celts would behave to warn people to stay away." "So, you do think it was Vortan?" said Tina. "Have you spoken to him about this," she said. "I haven't had chance," said Tim. "Also, he seems to be conspicuous by his silence since the event." "Perhaps I can get through to him later when things have calmed down." "OK," said Tina," I think we should leave you to rest now, the doctor said they were going to keep you over night to make sure that there were no ill effects from that bang on the head." She gave Tim big hug and stepped back while Hotpot put his hand on Tim's shoulder and said, "I'll see you tomorrow." Then Rebecca came over to the bed with tears in her eyes. "I'm so proud of you," she said as she wrapped her arms around him once more and nearly squeezed him to death.

After they'd all left and Tim was alone once more, he turned his thoughts to Vortan. "Well," he said, "what have you got to say for yourself?" There was no reply. "Come on I know you're there so don't pretend you're not," said Tim, scolding. "What do you want me to say?" came the reply from Vortan, unapologetically. "You killed those two men didn't you," said Tim sternly. "I killed those two men, yes, and if I hadn't, they would have killed you!" "Should I have let them do that instead?" said Vortan. "You could have stopped them without killing them, couldn't you?" said Tim. There was a silent pause, then Vortan spoke. "Those two men, along with fat Harold were ruthless criminals who would stop at nothing to get what they want." "They were warriors who lived by violence, it was their choice to live that way, so don't grieve for them." "They died as they lived!"

"What's more important is that many years ago I lost my life, my family and everything that I had, to thugs like that and I have no intention of letting that happen again!" "So, call me as much as you wish, if anybody threatens you or your family or friends, they had better be prepared for big trouble and I am not going to apologise for that, so get used to it!" said Vortan. Tim thought for a moment. "I understand what you say," said Tim, "but did you have to cut off their heads and stick them on poles like that?" "Well," said Vortan, "That's what we do, and it was a warning to others, not to try and harm you, so you should be glad I was there to protect you." "Anyway," said Vortan, "Fat Harold will get the blame for that because I put the sword in his hands, while he was unconscious, which is what he deserves; he caused all this trouble with his greed, so don't feel bad for him." "OK," said Tim, "but you know I hate all this violence don't you." "I know," said Vortan, "but you also know that when you behave passively with bullies, they get worse not better, don't they?" "I know that, very well," said Tim. "Anyway, I need to get some sleep now, so we'll talk about it some more tomorrow."

Tim fell asleep dreaming about his favourite place, the woods and grove where he first met Vortan, he was incredibly happy there despite all the recent troubles. When he awoke the next morning, it was early, and the nurse was checking up on him. She spent a few minutes with him and decided he was much improved on when he came in yesterday. "The doctor will be around to see you later and I think he will let you go home today," she said. "Good," said Tim.

He was having breakfast when Jack and Mary Bickerstaff came in to see him. After chatting with the policeman outside the room they came in. They couldn't decide whether to be happy that he was OK or feel guilty that they had brought all these problems on to him. Mary gave Tim the biggest hug; tears running down her face, she could hardly speak, she was so upset. Jack put his big powerful arms around both of them, also with tears in his eyes. "How are you?" asked Mary tearfully. "I'm fine!" said Tim. They were so relieved to see that Tim was looking so good. "I'm so sorry we got you into all this trouble," said Mary. "It's not your fault," said Tim. "You didn't do anything wrong," "Please don't blame yourselves for any of this, it's not your fault." "Anyway," said Tim, "How are you? The last time I saw you two, Harold was pointing a gun at you." "We're fine," said Jack.

Just then the door opened and in walked detective chief inspector Batley Bonus. "Good morning how are we all today?" he said in his deep voice. "We're fine," said Jack. "And I'm fine," said Tim. "And I'm going home today!" "Good," said the policeman, "If you wish, I'll take you home after you've seen the doctor," "OK," said Tim.

CHAPTER FORTY

BACK HOME

At home there was a party atmosphere. Tim's mum Tina, Rebecca, Hotpot, and the Bickerstaff's', they were all there. Also, Tim's granddad had travelled up to welcome him home from hospital. Rebecca was guarding him like a mother hen, sat on the couch next to him. Hotpot was sat on the arm of the couch. Chief inspector Bonus was getting rather fidgety because he wanted to question Tim, but it was obvious he wasn't going to be able to do that just now, so he decided to leave it to a later date. Tim's granddad wanted to know all about the goings on. The Bickerstaff's' were simply happy that Tim was all right. Mary had brought lots of fresh cakes that she had baked specially. It was an incredibly happy day, but Tim really wanted some time alone so he could question Vortan about yesterday's events. Vortan was happy it was so busy, and Tim couldn't quiz him about his violent behaviour. He didn't understand all the fuss, just because he'd killed a couple of enemy warriors and cut off their heads and stuck them on poles, just like he was used to doing. It was all very confusing for him. He was just protecting his people as he was trained to do. He decided to go and consult with his gods. He spoke to Tim inside his head told him what he wanted to do. "Where?" said Tim in return. "Our sacred grove, the Nemeton, the place where you first met me!" "OK," said Tim, but he said it out loud. "OK what?" said Rebecca. Tim laughed as he realised, he'd spoken out loud. "Oh nothing," he said smiling. After a while thing quietened down as all the visitors went home and Tim was left with just his mother Tina, and his granddad Edgar.

Tim went up to his room to rest, as suggested by his mother. As he was reflecting on the joyful day with his family and friends around him, he felt a familiar surge inside him. "You're back then!" Tim said to Vortan. "I'm back, and I'm sorry to have left you, but I wasn't far away, and I needed to consult the gods." "Oh, that again, said Tim. "And what did they tell you this time?" "They told me I was right to protect you and your friends." "Did they also say it was alright to kill those men and cut off their heads?" "That's just normal practice in my world," said Vortan. "Besides they were going to kill you and who knows what else; they are dangerous and desperate people." "Or at least they were until they had their heads cut off." "Now they're not dangerous anymore." "Apart from Harold that is, and he is the real problem, along with his wife." "They are greedy and nasty people, and we need to be aware of their intentions." "What do you propose?" said Tim. "Well, we don't have to worry about Fat Harold for the time being," said Vortan. "It's Big Harold," said Tim, "and why don't we have to worry about him?" "Well," said Vortan, "he is under arrest, and having difficulty explaining how he was found with the sword in his hand that cut off the heads of those two thugs." "Also, there is the small matter of the assault on you and kidnap, plus the business of carrying a gun and threatening the Bickerstaff's'." "All in all, I think we could say he has a few problems to deal with at the moment!"

"There is something else we must consider," said Vortan. "Fat Harold's wife Helen is still free and should not be underestimated!" "Why do you think that?" said Tim. "She's not as innocent as you think in all this," said Vortan. "Really," said Tim, "why do you think that?" "Because she is the real driving force, Harold may be the muscle and the frontman, but Helen is the brains behind his actions!" "She's clever and keeps herself out of harm's way, while her bully of a husband goes blundering in, like a bull," said Vortan. This gave Tim something to think about. "I must tell the Bickerstaff's 'To watch out for her!" Tim thought. "Time to rest now," said Tim.

CHAPTER FORTY-ONE

CELEBRATION

"Good idea!" said Vortan. "May I suggest that we do something together, in order to help you recover from all this violence and bad feelings of the past few days." "Sounds like a good idea," said Tim, what did you have in mind?" "Well, I thought we could recount my memory of a happy and joyful occasion, when lots of people came to visit our settlement for a big celebration." "Sounds brilliant," said Tim, "What was the occasion?" "It happened every year, at Midsummer, but one year when I was about your age, or perhaps a little younger, it was very special," said Vortan. "On this particular occasion, many great druids from faraway places travelled to be with us." "Not just druids, but many great warriors and tribal leaders, including my grandfather, King Erin and two other kings from the southern lands, some had spent many days, even weeks travelling, it was a very special occasion and we all spent weeks preparing for it." "Wow," said Tim that sounds really exiting, but what was the celebration actually for?" "Well, every year we celebrated midsummer sunrise and sunset, and in between there was feasting, partying, and lots of fun and games." "It was actually a thanksgiving to our gods, for their protection throughout the year, but everyone took the opportunity have lots of fun and meet up with old friends, make new friends." "It was also often a time for tribal leaders and important people to get together and make pacts or trade deals." "We were busy for a long time building temporary huts for the visitors in the field next to our settlement." "OK," said Vortan, "close your eyes and relax and let's see if we can reach into my memories of that occasion." Tim at once got pictures in his head. He was seeing through Vortan's eyes. He could see all the little children running around, some of them had bits of the warriors' blue paint on but not all over like the warriors wore. They had toy bows and arrows, toy spears and toy axes. They were playing hunting and war games. All the older boys and girls were helping with the preparations for the festivities.

Then the visions flicked to a different scene. Tim was looking at a group of warriors lining the pathway outside the village, they were not wearing war paint, but they were carrying spears. Tim, looking through Vortan's eyes was stood in the middle of the pathway with what he took to be Vortan's father, Etain. He was a large and imposing man, he was dressed, not in war mode but in best party dress. Heavy golden torque round his neck, golden bands on his upper arms. He was carrying a massive spear, at least seven feet long with a large shiny bronze head. It was also decorated all along the wooden shaft with carved and painted strange symbols. Etain was a fearsome looking man with big shoulders and big arms. He looked as if he could throw that spear right through the trunk of a tree. He was wearing a kind of leather pants and sandals. He had long blond hair like Vortan but many scars on his bare chest and arms plus the very obvious one on the left side of his face from his eye to his chin. He seemed to be quite proud of his scars, he certainly didn't try to hide them. Then some of the children started shouting and running to the side of the path squeezing in between the warriors that were lining the way.

They were excited because there was a party just arriving. First a group of six large warriors carrying spears, all dressed the same, brown animal skin pants, long red cloaks almost touching the floor, mocker sans or sandals. Next three men in white robes, Tim took to be Druids, all carrying long staffs, two with white beards, the other clean shaven and completely bald, all quite old. Then came horsemen, firstly, a lone rider, dressed in exceptionally fine clothes, a long white cloak, a heavy golden torque around his neck, a large bronze sword with a beautiful golden handle beset with jewels and gemstones slotted into his saddle. He was quite old, but he looked very important. He was very tanned with grey hair. Behind him came two women on horseback, dressed in fine brightly coloured dresses with long cloaks, one white and one blue. The one in white was wearing lots of gold and jewels, a beautiful golden torque round her neck, golden bangles on her wrists. Even bangles on her ankles. Then came many horsemen; warriors all dressed the same with red cloaks. All carrying spears, all with bronze swords slotted into their saddles. There were dozens of them, they looked absolutely magnificent. After the horsemen came dozens more warriors, on foot, some with long bows, and some with spears.

As the first warriors approached, Etain, then Vortan, stepped out to greet them. Etain went to the first two warriors, who looked remarkably like him with long blonde hair and similar facial features, also with similar physiques: broad shoulders and big arms. They both greeted Etain with big hugs. It turned out that they were his younger brothers. He then greeted the other four of the first group. They were obviously great friends. Vortan was picked up by one of his uncles and hoisted in the air at arm's length, then as he was put down the other uncle gave him a big hug. Etain then stepped up to the three druids and greeted them with a hand on the shoulder. He then passed to his father, King Erin. The king reached down and took his hand and smiled. Etain took hold of his father's horse and led it the short distance to the settlement. All the children fallowed jumping about and cheering waving their toy weapons. When they reached the settlement, only the first six warriors, the three druids, the king and the two ladies crossed the bridge into the compound. The rest of the party were led to the newly constructed huts, where they were treated to refreshing drinks and food.

Across the bridge in the compound, Etain held the kings' horse while he dismounted and gave him a hug. He then went to the lady in white and lifted her off her horse and gave her the biggest hug; it was his mother, Queen Morrigu. The young Vortan helped the other lady off her horse. Merva was waiting to greet the king and his party. The king dismounted, the six forward guards formed a pathway as the king smiled and walked towards Merva. She smiled and held out her hands to great her husbands' father the king. He took her hands, then they embraced. The strange thing was that Merva didn't bow her head and the king seemed to be just as honoured to greet Merva as Merva was to greet the king. Then the king turned to the young Vortan, who was not so tall at this time; the king was a noticeably big man, he picked Vortan up and held him above his head, then put him down and gave him a big hug. Tim felt very strange experiencing all this royal family stuff, but it was very exciting. Merva, after greeting the king and the two ladies, who was obviously The Queen, (Morrigu) and her lady in waiting, (Tippi), turned to the three druids, who had been waiting patiently, they all seemed to be very honoured to be in her company. They waited in turn while she held out both her hands to each of them in turn. Then Merva turned to her husband's two brothers, (Ceanach) and (Cumhaill). They were both famous warriors and Tim thought what they might look like in their war paint, charging into battle. "Best not think about it," he said to himself. It was a wonderful occasion though, and everyone was having a great time.

Over the next few days' people arrived from all over the land. Sometimes in groups like King Erin's and sometimes just small numbers, and sometimes just individuals. Eventually there were three kings with their full entourages and more than twenty Druids and lots of other important people. It was the most incredible and colourful occasion with the kings and their families wearing all their finery; lots of gold and precious stones. Also to see so many druids all together was a rare sight. All in all, it was a very special occasion and a wonderful sight.

Tim's next vision was of a grand procession, morning time at down. The grass was soaking wet with a heavy dew. At the head of the procession was Merva in her usual immaculate white robe. She was also wearing a beautiful golden torque around her neck. Her shiny black hair reached down past her waist, and she was carrying a long wooden staff, carved and painted with strange patterns, it also had a white carved head of a strange looking creature on the top. She was followed closely by a whole group of white robed druids, some of them females, but all dressed the same, walking two abreast. Then came King Erin and two other kings, all walking together. Next came Queen Morrigu and two other queens, followed by their ladies in waiting. Vortan and his farther, Etain came next, followed by Etain's two brothers Ceanach and Cumhail. They all looked magnificent in their best finery and especially their bright red cloaks, but this time none of the warriors, including King Erin and the other kings were carrying weapons. It was a spiritual gathering and weapons were neither necessary nor welcome. The procession tailed all the way back from the sacred grove to the settlement and included everyone in the tribe and all those who had travelled with the visitors.

When Vortan's group arrived in the grove they took their place behind the stone alter, which was laden with several large earthenware jugs and many drinking cups, plus a giant plate with fruit on. Merva was in front of the alter welcoming everyone as they arrived. The last to arrive was the mothers with their children. Merva told all the children to come to the front and sit down on the logs. The grove was absolutely crowded and as the sun started to come up the whole party turned to face the east and watch as it came up over the arisen. When it was completely above the arisen Merva held her hands and arms up to the heavens and said a prayer for a few moments, then turned and blessed all the contents of the alter. After a few more prayers, a group of white robed teenaged girls came forward and proceeded to pour out drinks from the large jugs into cups and pass them out to everyone in the grove. As all this was going on, the druids started singing a gentle song and everyone else started joining in the singing. Tim thought, what a beautiful and happy vision, as a very warm feeling spread over him. "I feel wonderful, thank you for that Vortan, I would like to see some more of that some time." It also occurred to Tim that his favourite place, the grove in Tarbock Wood, had been in the past, a particularly important and spiritual place, a place of real magic. It's no wonder that he felt very strange whenever he was in there. I think it's time for sleep now. "Good!" said Vortan.

To be continued...